THE VAMPIRE WHO CAME FOR CHRISTMAS

Also by Dian Curtis Regan:

My Zombie Valentine
The Kissing Contest
Liver Cookies

THE VAMPIRE WHO CAME FOR CHRISTMAS

Dian Curtis Regan

AN
APPLE
PAPERBACK

SCHOLASTIC INC.
New York Toronto London Auckland Sydney

No part of this publication may be reproduced in whole or in part, or stored in a retrieval system, or transmitted in any form or by any means, electronic, mechanical, photocopying, recording, or otherwise, without written permission of the publisher. For information regarding permission, write to Scholastic Inc., 730 Broadway, New York, NY 10003.

ISBN 0-590-47862-1

12 11 10 9 8 7 6 5 4 3   3 4 5 6 7 8/9

Printed in the U.S.A.   40

First Scholastic printing, November 1993

This book is dead-icated to three fiends who expired me:
Cindy Knox, Darleen Bailey Beard,
Pati Hailey Vloedman

Contents

1. Things That Go Bump in the Attic   1
2. V.A.M.P.   10
3. Hearts of Frog on Lettuce   17
4. Exterminator Juice   26
5. Show Me Christmas   31
6. Deck the Halls with Boughs of Horror   38
7. Fangs for the Memories   47
8. A Hawk and a Thorn   53
9. Reverse the Curse   59
10. The Seventh Son   66
11. Hark! The Comic Vampire Comes   74
12. Silent Night, Scary Night   84
13. The Wrath of The Big Guy   91
14. Silver Fangs, Silver Fangs, Soon It Will Be Christmas Day   100
15. It's Beginning to Look a Lot Like Curtains   111

THE VAMPIRE WHO CAME FOR CHRISTMAS

1.
Things That Go
Bump in the Attic

"Isn't it too late in the year for squirrels?" Ben Garcia asked, printing his name in steam fogging the kitchen window.

"Well, *something's* making a racket in the attic." His mother peeked into the oven. "When I went up to get Christmas decorations, I unlatched the shutter over that broken window for light. Guess I left it open." She added five minutes to the timer.

Cinnamon-flavored air teased Ben's nose. "Another project to add to your list," he told her. "Fix broken window."

"Right, and get an electrician to run wires up there for a light." Mom loaded the ancient dishwasher. "Please go up and chase out the squirrel?"

Ben would rather have stayed at the table, waiting for a warm turnover. Besides, he was almost finished writing his history report on "The President's Cabinet." But Christmas was next week.

He'd better make a good impression on Mom by doing things the *first* time she asked.

Shutting his history book, he headed for the attic stairs tucked behind the pantry. "Trade you a squirrel for a turnover," he teased.

"Don't you dare bring that thing down here," Mom yelped. "And the turnovers are promised to the Volunteers' church supper."

Ben paused to help peeling paint remove itself from the pantry door. "No one will notice if one turnover's missing. . . ."

"I guess not." Mom pounded on top of the dishwasher to make it start. "But hurry if you want it warm; they're almost done."

Ben took the rickety stairs two at a time — always afraid they might collapse before he made it to the attic door. His black cat, Licorice, appeared from nowhere, zooming up the steps in front of him.

To her, the attic playground held lots of surprises: spiders, moths, field mice — and squirrels.

"Ready to go hunting?" He opened the attic door.

Darkness swallowed the cat.

Ben gulped, stopping before the last step. He didn't like spooky, spiderwebby places. Who did? Yet, the sooner he chased out the squirrel, the sooner he'd bite into that warm cinnamon turnover.

His family had moved to the old Canfield house on Meadow Lane in Woodrock three months ago. After living in the city, Ben loved the generous backyard, edged by a forest. But the house seemed to have its share of broken shutters and boards, shaky places and spaces.

"A real fixer-upper," his mom had called it. Her real estate business included buying old houses and making them almost-new again. Then reselling, moving, and starting over on another "find."

But this time she'd picked a doozie; they might be here a while. Okay with Ben. He liked his school, especially the music teacher Ms. Sasaki, who'd chosen him lead vocalist for the Christmas program.

He pictured himself singing his solo to the audience, catching the proud look on his parents' faces. . . .

Quit stalling, Garcia.

"Okay, okay," Ben whispered, answering his conscience.

He took the last creaky step. In his rush, he'd forgotten the flashlight stashed at the bottom of the stairwell. A shaft of twilight from the open shutter lit a hazy path for him to follow.

The air smelled like damp cardboard, hundred-year-old dust, and musty mildew. Not a pleasant aroma.

3

"Ouch," he mumbled, tripping over boxes. His parents had been too busy to finish unpacking. Storing stuff in the attic offered an easy solution.

Licorice hunched on a stack of boxes, waiting for Ben to find the squirrel so she could move in and terrorize it.

"Thanks, Lic," he said. "You're a big help."

Winding his way to the broken window, Ben opened it to give the squirrel an easy exit. Then he scouted the dusty floor for tiny tracks.

As he knelt, a noisy rustling from the far side of the attic brought him to his feet. *It's only the squirrel,* he told himself. Still, being here in the dusky light with strange noises was creepy.

He glanced at Licorice. Her back curved in a raised-hair arch; her eyes gleamed gold-green. Her puffed-out tail was the size of a baseball bat. A second later, she streaked to the door and down the stairs, leaving an eerie wail as her calling card.

The foreboding cat-cry unnerved Ben. "Must be a *big* squirrel."

He circled the attic, flinching at every squeak of the floorboards. "Here boy," he called. "H-e-e-e-re, boy."

"*Why* are you calling me 'boy'?" came a thickly accented voice from the darkest corner. "And pre-

4

cisely what is it you want me to do?"

Ben gasped. His skin prickled. Every hair on his body fluffed like Licorice's tail. "Who . . . who . . . who . . . ?"

"Don't address me as though I'm an owl," came the voice. "And the question is — who are *you?* And why are you in my house?"

Ben's mind roller-coastered. Who *was* this? A homeless person seeking shelter? A burglar? Or worse? His mother was downstairs alone, his dad, on the road again. *He* was in charge.

"Look, mister." Ben's voice quivered from fear. "This isn't your house. *My* family lives here. You'd better get out — whoever you are."

His threat met silence.

"Um, hello?" Twilight had traded places with moonlight, making it harder to see. "Look, if you don't leave right now, I'll yell for my father," he bluffed. "And my brothers."

No answer.

"My uncles and grandfathers, too." Ben hoped the threat of attack by the entire Garcia family would work, even though his father was in Akron, he didn't have any brothers, and his uncles and grandfathers were scattered up and down the West Coast.

More rustling from the corner. "How could you have moved in without my hearing it?" The voice sounded flustered. "I have *exceptional* hearing; we *all* do, and I've only been asleep a short time, so — "

"Ben!" His mother's voice echoed up the stairway. "Are you having any luck up there with Sammy?"

"Sammy?" the man repeated.

"Sammy" was the name tacked onto all four-legged intruders in the attic. "He's just leaving!" Ben hollered back.

Good. Now this guy thinks there's a whole bunch of people downstairs, so he'd better —

"I left your dessert on the table," Mom called. "I'm off to the church. Keep the doors locked while you're alone, and do your homework."

Great. Tell the stranger I'm alone. Ben tried to keep the word *murderer* from tiptoeing into his mind.

The front door slammed, then the engine in Mom's realtor "tank" raced like a fighter jet's as she drove away.

Ben backed toward the stairs. Maybe he could bolt down them like Licorice and dash for help. Too bad the nearest house was Marly Thorn's — the last person on earth he'd choose to run to.

"Well, I'm sorry you've discovered me," the man said in a voice that *sounded* sorry. "I'll simply do my job, then be on my way. Now that it's dark, I can — "

"Your *job?*"

The rustling noise skirted the boxes, moving closer.

In the hazy light, Ben saw the outline of a tall figure, wearing a flowing cape with a stand-up collar. As the figure approached, moonlight dusted his face. He was pale. Paler than anyone Ben had ever seen.

His nose was thin, his bushy eyebrows met in the middle, and his ears had definite points to them.

He gave an elegant bow. "I believe we need to be properly introduced since you've called me *boy* and *Sammy,* neither of which are correct. My name is Alexander Carpathian. And you are Benjamin, although your mother called you Ben. Am I correct?"

"Y-Yes." Ben was calculating the man's height. Seven feet? Was it possible? Staring up at the moon-white face put a crick in his neck.

"I will call you Benjamin," he said. "It's more formal and proper. You may call me Zander. That's what my friends call me, and I *do* hope we'll be friends." He extended a gloved hand.

The last thing Ben wanted was to shake his hand, but he didn't want to appear impolite since the man seemed to have such good manners.

Gingerly, he reached for the stranger's hand.

7

It felt as cold as the stone wall surrounding the garden out back. Even through the glove.

Ben yanked away, trying to ignore the chills tidal-waving through him. "Why are you dressed like that?"

"Well, tonight's the big night. All Hallow's Eve. Time to dress up and stroll beneath the harvest moon. You, I presume, are going out, also?"

"What are you talking about? Tonight isn't Halloween."

"Well, of course it is; don't be silly. It's my job to know these things."

This guy is weird. Weird without a calendar. "Oh, I get it," Ben said. "You *think* tonight is Halloween, so you're going out dressed as a . . . a vampire?"

The man was amused. Even his laughter was heavily accented. And it went on and on and *on*, from one octave to another. Like this:

"Ha   ha   ha!"
       ha   ha   ha   ha
          ha   ha   ha   ha
             ha   ha

"What's so funny?" Ben was confused. *Did I miss something?*

"My dear Benjamin," the man said with a final chuckle. "Tonight *is* Halloween. And I am not simply *dressed* as a vampire." He paused to swirl his cape impressively over one shoulder. "I *am* a vampire."

2.
V.A.M.P.

"You . . . you . . . you . . ." was all Ben could
stammer.

A real vampire? his mind screamed. *The kind
that bites your neck and drinks your blood? The
kind that kills you? Or turns you into a vampire,
too?*

The man grinned. Moonlight glinted off his
teeth. Especially the two that were longer than
the rest. And sharper. And pointier.

"I . . . I . . . I . . ." Ben wrapped a hand
around his throat in an attempt to protect himself.

"Oh!" the vampire exclaimed. "I've frightened
you." Instantly his pointy fangs receded, blending
in with his other teeth.

Ben was fascinated in spite of the danger.

The man dropped to one knee to talk to Ben
eye to eye. "Please forgive me," he said. "I was
not trying to scare you; I was simply trying to
convince you that I am who I say I am."

He gripped Ben by the shoulders. "Do you believe me now?"

"Y-Y-Yes," Ben stuttered. Was he doomed? He tried to picture his life flashing in front of his eyes, but it was far too short to make much of a video.

Why didn't I run when I had the chance?

Now the man held him in an icy grip. Closing his eyes, Ben waited to feel sharp fangs sink into the tender flesh of his neck. *Good-bye, Benjamin Avery Garcia. I love you, Mom. And Dad. And Licorice. And Ms. Sasaki.*

"Are you all right?" The vampire gave his shoulders a shake.

Ben opened his eyes. "Well?" he asked. "Aren't you going to — ?"

"To what?"

"*You* know." *Do I have to tell a vampire how to do his job?*

"You mean — ." He let go. "You think — ? Ah ha, ha, ha." Then:

"Ha   ha   ha!"
   ha   ha   ha   ha
      ha   ha   ha   ha
        ha   ha

Groaning, Ben took three giant steps backward. He was safe. For now.

"My dear boy, I am not going to hurt you. That

would be very impolite of me, wouldn't it? I'm not going to bite your neck, nor your mother's or father's or brothers' or uncles' or grandfathers'."

"You're not?" Relieved, Ben thought of Hawk Riley, his tormenter at Rollingwood Middle School. Maybe he could give Hawk's address to the vampire, and . . .

"No, no, no," the man continued. "I'm not *that* kind of vampire. As a matter of fact, I'm a member of an organization in *favor* of the protection of humans, and *against* the drinking of real blood. We — the members of V.A.M.P. — Vampires Against Mutilating People — live a different kind of life than those . . . those *other* kind of vampires."

"Really?" The news disappointed him. It was like finding out Santa's elves knew nothing about building toys so they ordered them all from the J.C. Penney catalog.

"So, um . . . Zander. What are you doing in my attic? And why do you think it's Halloween?"

The man sat back on his haunches and raised an eyebrow. "Haven't we been through this already?"

"But — " *How can I convince him it's December — not October?* "Come here," Ben said, following the moonlit path to the window.

Zander, cape rustling, followed.

"Look."

"Look at what?"

"The backyard. What do you see?"

"I see — snow?"

"Right. If it was October, you'd see leaves on the ground, not snow. Not in this part of the country."

Zander was silent.

"And look at the trees."

"My goodness, they're bare."

"Right. No red-and-gold leaves. They've all fallen and died."

"What's that?" Zander pointed to a brightly lit house in the distance.

"Christmas lights."

"What are Christmas lights?"

I don't believe I'm having this conversation. With a vampire, no less.

"Everyone packed away Halloween costumes weeks ago. Now people are decorating their homes for Christmas."

The vampire's pale face grew even paler. He backed away from the window, knocking over boxes. "Oh, it's *true*. I've overslept. Halloween has passed, and I've missed my assignment."

He twirled toward Ben, cape flapping about him like wings. "Do you know what this means?"

"No, I — "

"Mith, mith, *mith*, what have I done?"

"Mith?" Ben repeated.

"Oh, I'm sorry. Your tender ears. I must watch my language. *Mith* means . . . well . . . it's not a very nice word back in Multiveinia."

"Multiveinia?"

"Yes. My home. Oh, will I ever see home again? Now that I've messed up my assignment?"

Zander headed back into the dark corner of the attic. "How? What? When?" he muttered. "He's going to murder me — well, if he *could*, he'd murder me." He glanced at Ben. "That's the problem with being immortal; they can torment you for centuries, but cannot kill you."

"Wow. You've been alive for centuries?"

"Since 1643."

1643. Ben tried to imagine being alive over 300 years ago. Weren't the pilgrims just settling the colonies then? "Wow," he repeated as he watched the vampire riffle through what looked like a traveling bag.

Ben had a million questions. "Who are *they?* And what was your assignment? And what are they going to do to you?"

Zander stopped to explain. "I'm not worried about *them*, I'm worried about *him*. The Big Guy. It's what *he* will do to me."

"The Big Guy?"

"Yes, in Multiveinia. He's the Czar of all Vampires. The King of the Undead. The Emperor of Doom. The Count of Ghastly Castle."

"Cool. What's his name?"

"He's so powerful, if I said his name to you, you'd melt into a puddle. A Benjamin puddle. I don't even *know* his name. That's how powerful it is. We — the VAMPs — call him The Big Guy. And you *never* break his rules, which I've managed to do by oversleeping."

Zander reached into his bag and pulled out two boxes. "Ah, here are the culprits. I have terrible allergies when I visit this part of the world. I guess I took too much Anti-hearse-tamine and extra-strength Allerbled. Oh, how could I have been so careless?" A tear rolled down his cheek. "I may never see my wife or kids again."

"You have a wife and kids?" Ben was astounded. *A vampire with a home life?*

"Oh, yes. Waiting for my return to Multiveinia. Layla, beautiful Layla. And the twins, Zander Junior and Zandra."

"Those are your kids' names?" Ben swallowed a laugh.

The vampire began to pace. His cape swirled with every turn. "You've got to help me, Benjamin."

"Me?"

"Yes. When The Big Guy finds out I skipped Halloween, he'll come here to find out why."

"Here? To my house?" Ben's next question was one he was afraid to ask: "Is he a member of

V.A.M.P.? Or is he one of those *other* kind of vampires? The kind who bites and drinks?"

"He bites and drinks," Zander said. "Doesn't even bother to ask your name first. Has no manners at all. And he's outraged about V.A.M.P. If he finds out I'm involved . . ."

"Can't you just *go?* Disappear? Pick up your family and leave no forwarding address?"

"Unfortunately, I can move only when and where he tells me. My assignments, in case you haven't guessed, are to seek out and terrorize victims. But instead, my V.A.M.P. colleagues and I spread peace and love. The Big Guy hasn't figured it all out yet, but he *does* track our movements, so he knows I'm still here. My next assignment must have come while I was sleeping, so I don't know where I'm supposed to be right now."

"You mean —"

"Yes, I'm stuck here. With you."

"Until?"

"Until The Big Guy comes to find out why, or . . ."

"Or what?"

"Or *you* come up with a plan."

3.
Hearts of Frog on Lettuce

Ben hunched in his seat on the school bus, pretending to read his history book because he didn't feel like talking to anyone.

Plus, he hadn't finished writing his history report last night. The vampire kept him in the attic moaning and groaning about his plight until Mom's car pulled into the driveway at ten o'clock.

The vampire.

Ben still had to bonk himself on the head to believe he'd actually spent the evening with a *real* vampire. A very polite creature who did not believe in killing. Or in drinking real blood.

Zander had shown him VAMP's *One Vein; One World* catalog, from which he ordered monthly supplies of *simulated* blood, mixed with pure herbal ingredients. The imitation blood was sugar-free, fat-free, salt-free, and made without animal testing.

Ben thought it sounded like "Blood Lite."

17

He felt thankful this vampire was a reformed one, with a penchant for spreading life instead of death. If not, the Garcia family would be doomed.

Marly Thorn sat next to him, humming "The Twelve Days of Christmas." She was only up to day four, but her staccato "Mm-mm-mm-mm-mms" were driving Ben crazy.

If he hadn't been so preoccupied when he boarded the bus, he wouldn't have taken an empty seat. Every time he did, Marly slid in beside him, then pestered him all the way to school.

He glared at her as she hummed "five go-o-o-lden rings." Only it sounded like "Mmmm-Mm-m-m-Mm-Mmmmm."

Holding the last note of her hum, she smiled at his glare, raising her eyebrows in question. "What?" she asked, leaning close as if he was about to whisper a deep, dark secret. Her foofy blonde hair fell onto his shoulder.

"Would you please shut up, Thorn? I'm trying to concentrate."

"Don't get mad at *me* because you didn't finish your history report."

He shoved his notebook in her face. "Look what you made me write."

Marly deliberately placed her hand over his to grasp the notebook.

Disgusted, he yanked his hand away.

She held up the page and read out loud, "The

President appoints thirteen pears to head each department in his Cabinet. Ha!" she laughed. "You wrote *pears* instead of *people*."

"I wonder why." Ben snatched his paper back, humming "and a partridge in a pear tree" as loudly as he could three inches from her ear.

The instant he got to homeroom, Ben scribbled the end of his report — not in his best handwriting. He'd planned to list the current Cabinet members, but there hadn't been time to find all the names — or type his paper on Mom's computer, thanks to the Garcias' new house guest.

During the next fifteen minutes, Mr. Rosetti called roll, kids settled in, and those who remembered to bring Christmas ornaments from home hung them on a fake tree, listing dangerously to one side in the corner.

What Ben did was think about last night: How he'd calmed Zander, making him promise to be quiet so Mom wouldn't suspect another squirrel.

How they'd brainstormed ways to keep The Big Guy from finding Zander. Ben's best idea — stringing garlic cloves around the attic — was quickly shot down after Zander pointed out that the garlic would repel *him* as well as the King of the Undead. *Whoops.*

Ben thought about how he'd raced downstairs when he heard his mom's car, and how he'd found half the forgotten turnover next to his homework. A trail of powdered sugar told him Licorice had helped herself to his dessert. He'd trashed the rest seconds before Mom walked in.

The last thing Ben thought about was Zander's questions about Christmas. He'd taken Zander downstairs to the den, and showed him how to operate the VCR and TV so he could watch Dad's collection of Christmas videos today while the house was empty. With the drapes pulled, the den was as dark as the attic.

Showing the vampire what to do was the easy part. The hard part was explaining how those "little people got inside the box."

And the worrisome part was hoping Zander finished the videos and made it back to the attic before Mom came home from work this afternoon.

"Mr. Garcia, why are you still wearing your jacket?"

Ben jumped. Mr. Rosetti, in his quiet running shoes, had come up the aisle from behind.

"Um, I didn't have time to go to my locker." He didn't want to explain further since Mr. Rosetti was also his history teacher. Ben didn't want him to know that the history report had received less than his best effort.

In music class, everyone was hyper. The Christmas program was Friday night, yet parts of the concert were still pretty shaky. Like the medley of Christmas songs no one had heard before.

Songs with titles like: "Thou Doth Watcheth Over Thee." That one made the entire choir sound like a flock of Daffy Ducks, lisping through the lyrics.

The best part of the program, in Ben's mind, was his solo. He'd spent hours rehearsing, alone and with Ms. Sasaki. He knew his voice was good. Friday would be the first time he'd sung alone in front of an audience.

The thought thrilled him and terrified him at the same time.

The *worst* part about the program was his place on the risers. Tallest in back; shortest in front. He wasn't tall enough for the top row in the tenor section, so, positioned right behind him was Hawk Riley, a guy who made Marly Thorn seem like Ben's best friend.

"People!" Ms. Sasaki yelled to get everyone's attention. Her voice was as tiny as she was, so her yell wasn't all that loud. "Thank you for quieting down and taking your places."

She always said that before they quieted down or took their places, but somehow it made everyone do just that.

"Let's pretend it's the big night."

She always said that, too, as if it would make their voices perfect, instead of wobbly, as usual.

"I want you to give it your best," she continued. "Take it from the top, and go right through the program without stopping. Pretend your parents are sitting here listening."

Ben watched Ms. Sasaki step up on a chair so everyone in back could see her. The teacher's dark hair was caught up on one side in a ponytail, making her look like one of the sixth-grade girls.

Pre-taped music began, and the choir launched into "It's Beginning to Look a Lot Like Christmas," but before they segued into "Silver Bells," Marly Thorn threw her hand in the air, waving in time to the music.

Ms. Sasaki gave a brisk shake of her head, flipping her ponytail back and forth. It meant, *Marly put your hand down*, but Marly kept waving.

Finally, the teacher made a slicing motion across her neck. The choir groaned to a slow-motion stop, sounding like a cassette player with dying batteries. "Marly, what is it? Performers *always* keep going, no matter what happens. The show comes first."

"But Hawk keeps cracking his knuckles. It's throwing me off beat."

Snickers reverberated around the risers. The knuckle popping was annoying Ben, too, but he knew better than to tattle on The Hawk.

"Richard Riley," was all Ms. Sasaki had to say

22

to make him stop. Kids liked her, and didn't buck her too much. Even Hawk.

"Let's take it again, from the top."

They started once more, this time making it through the opening medley, the Daffy Duck lisp song, and to Ben's big moment.

While a dulcimer played the intro to his solo, the room temperature seemed to jump twenty degrees. Ben began to sweat. "O holy night," he sang, his voice breathy from nerves, "the stars are brightly shining. . . ."

At that point, Hawk began drumming between Ben's shoulder blades, making up a different beat that did not jibe with the carol.

Ben made it to the "weary world rejoices" before Hawk's drumming threw off his rhythm. From the third step of the risers, he could read disappointment in Ms. Sasaki's eyes.

He stopped singing. Groans echoed around him.

The teacher clicked off the tape. "Ben, your voice sounded so lovely last time we rehearsed. Is everything okay?"

"Um, yeah. I'm just . . . I'm just having a weird day. Sorry."

" 'I'm just having a weird day,' " Hawk mimicked under his breath.

Ben would've loved to pin the blame on the one who deserved it, but he'd already made that mistake his first day at Rollingwood. No one warned him about Hawk, but then why would they? Ben was just the "new guy."

It happened in biology lab. After sketching the inner organs of the frogs they'd dissected, each group was supposed to place their frog in a plastic tray to store in the refrigerator for the next day's experiment.

The teacher, Mrs. Petri, asked Ben to hand out trays. Meanwhile, Hawk extracted the heart from Ben's poor frog and flung it toward Mrs. Petri's desk. The heart landed right in the middle of the salad she'd just uncovered for lunch.

Mrs. Petri gave Ben an F for the day, so he spoke up, and Hawk got the F instead. In return, Ben had gotten Hawk on his case ever since.

For the rest of choir practice, Ben could barely join in the singing. Now Hawk had him worried. *What if he messes up my solo the night of the program? What if he humiliates me in front of my parents and Ms. Sasaki?*

Suddenly the words they were singing, "He's making a list and checking it twice," made Ben think of another solution to Zander's problem. If The Big Guy showed up, maybe Ben could entice Hawk to the attic while he and Zander made themselves scarce. One bite of Hawk's neck, and . . .

But, his conscience argued, *what if Hawk re-*

turns as a vampire and comes after ME? Ben couldn't imagine Hawk joining V.A.M.P. to spread peace and love. No, he'd be one of those *other* kind of vampires.

Ben shook the unsettling thoughts from his mind, halfheartedly joining in on the last chorus of "Santa Claus Is Coming to Town."

Maybe wishing The Big Guy's wrath on his worst enemy wasn't such a great idea after all.

4.
Exterminator Juice

Ben leaped from the school bus the second it stopped.

He dashed down Meadow Lane and into the house, dumped his books on the sofa, then headed for the attic stairs.

Licorice, waking from her nap in a window seat, usually shadowed him after school, begging for attention. But today, she followed as far as the pantry, then dashed in the other direction when she saw where Ben was going.

Now he knew what had caused her to freak last night.

Stopping at the top of the stairs to catch his breath, Ben's mind registered the fact that his mom was already home from the office. He'd heard her talking on the phone in the den.

I should have said hello so she won't suspect anything. He'd better make up a few good reasons for being in the attic.

Stepping into the darkness, he waited for his eyes to adjust. Wait a minute. Something was wrong. A light flickered behind a stack of boxes. *Don't vampires prefer darkness over light?*

He tiptoed around the boxes. A figure hunched against the back wall. "Zander?" Ben called, his voice sounding loud in the stillness.

The figure leaped into the air with a shriek as the light went out.

The shriek turned Ben's knees to soft clay. "Z-Z-Zander? Don't scare me every time I come to the attic."

"Who's Zander?" a voice said as a flashlight clicked on. "I'm Mildred."

They stared at each other. Ben knew vampires could shape-change, but why change into a middle-aged woman in too-big overalls?

"Who are *you?*" Ben was afraid to call her Zander again.

"I'm the electrician — peacefully wiring a light fixture until you crept up and scared the livin' breath out of me."

Ben read the logo on her overalls:

MILDRED'S ELECTRIC SUPPLY
LET ME FIX YOUR SHORTS

"Excuse me," Ben said, trying to be polite. "I didn't mean to startle you." His gaze danced around the attic. Where was Zander? Had Mildred seen him? Probably not, or she'd be shrieking even louder.

"Well, if you don't mind," the woman said, "I'm going to finish my job. And you can make yourself scarce." She returned to the bouquet of wires blooming from a two-by-four on the wall.

Ben headed toward Zander's dark corner. Maybe the vampire was hiding behind a box.

"Hold it," Mildred ordered.

Ben stopped.

"Don't go back there."

"Why not?"

"A bat got inside. He's hanging on a rafter. Didn't like it when I turned my flashlight on him, so now he's angry. Those things can attack and bite, and get so tangled up in your hair you have to cut them out."

She snapped a cable with wire cutters to make her point. "Better tell your mom so she can call Pest Control. One squirt of exterminator juice, and that bat will be a goner."

A bat. Ben's mind zoomed through all the vampire stories he'd read. *Of course. A bat.* No wonder they hadn't seen Zander when they moved in. He was asleep all right. But not in human form. He was hanging upside-down from a rafter in the darkest corner. A vampire bat.

Suddenly the rest of the lady's words sunk in.

Exterminator juice. One squirt. The bat will be a goner. *Oh, no. If The Big Guy doesn't get Zander, Mildred's mouth will. I'll have to keep her from telling Mom.*

"Ben, are you up there?" came his mother's voice, almost on cue.

"Yes!" *Please don't come up.* He rushed to the top of the stairs.

"Are you bothering the electrician?"

"No."

"Mildred, is he bothering you?"

"Yes."

"Be-en." Footsteps echoed in the stairwell. His mother was coming up! Which meant Mildred would mention the bat. Which meant . . .

Ben dashed down the steps, intercepting her. "When will Dad be home? Aren't we getting our Christmas tree tonight?"

His mother started around him, then stopped. "Oh, Ben, that was your father on the phone. He's not coming in tonight."

"He's not?" Panic gave way to disappointment. Not only did he miss his dad, but the three of them always went tree hunting together. "By the time we get our tree," he grumbled, "Christmas will be over."

Mom straightened his hair. How she could tell in the dark stairwell that his hair was messed up, he didn't know. "Dad said to tell you he's sorry, but one of the acts in Altoona cancelled, and he's flying in to replace them."

Ben shrugged. Akron, Altoona — didn't matter. Dad was always flying off somewhere.

"You and I can get a tree by ourselves," Mom said in a zippy voice, as if that would make him feel better. "We'll go after dinner, but only if your homework's done." She started up the stairs again.

Ben put both hands on the railings, blocking her way. "Then I really, really need your advice on my homework. Right now."

She hesitated. "Well, okay." Leaning around him, she hollered up the stairs. "Mildred! Call me if you need any help."

"You already helped me more than you know," Mildred hollered back.

Ben absorbed the insult. *What a grouch. Hates kids. And bats minding their own business.*

Oh, well, he didn't care. At least he'd made the electrician forget to recommend Pest Control.

"You owe me one, Zan," he whispered as he followed his mother through the pantry. "I just saved your hide. The winged, fuzzy version, that is."

5.
Show Me Christmas

As his mother waited, Ben shuffled through the school papers in his backpack. Oh, great. He didn't *have* homework tonight. Thinking fast, he came up with an assignment Mom could help him with — listening to his solo.

It wasn't a fib. Ms. Sasaki had told him to practice tonight, preferably with an audience. Mothers made the best kind of audience. His mom would never say he was awful, even if he was. But Ben knew he was never awful.

He sang until Mildred came down from the attic.

"Well, guess I'll take a break," he said, trying to sound nonchalant as Mom looked for the checkbook. "Think I'll go up and try out the new light."

"Hurry up," Mom told him. "If we're going to find a tree and get it decorated before midnight, we need to eat and leave."

Mildred glowered at Ben, either because he was distracting his mom from writing the check, or because she suspected he was rushing upstairs to make sure she'd done her job right.

If Mom wasn't around, Ben would've been tempted to say, "Why, Mildred, for an electrician, you're quite a shock." Ha, ha, ha. But he was afraid Mom — or Mildred — might ground him.

Instead, he bolted to the attic. "Zan, you can come out now. She's gone."

Ben flipped on the newly wired light and stepped across the room, squinting into the rafters, searching for an upside-down vampire bat.

The light clicked off. He whirled. Zander, in human form, loomed by the light switch. "Could we leave this off, please?"

Ben felt relieved to see him there, acting like himself. Mildred hadn't permanently injured him with her glaring flashlight after all. An open shutter let in enough light for Ben to see.

For a moment, the vampire didn't speak. Then he moved toward Ben and settled onto a box, cape fluttering around him as if it had a life of its own. Dropping his head into his hands, he began to sob.

"What's wrong?" Ben was at his side in an instant, awkwardly patting the vampire's shoulder. "We'll figure out a way to foil The Big Guy. Don't worry. We — "

"No, no, dear boy," Zander said between sniffles. "It's not that. I just heard you singing that lovely, lovely song downstairs, and it . . . well, it got me right here." He placed a gloved hand over his heart.

"You heard me singing?" Ben was pleased.

"You have a gift, son. You must pursue your music."

"Really?" Ben was thrilled. *He* knew he was good, but he wanted people — other than his mother — to notice. "My singing made you cry?"

"Your singing — and those dear, dear people in your father's videos. Little Tiny Tim. Why, if I'd known Scrooge, I'd have given him what he deserved after being mean to that poor boy's family. In those days, I was the *other* kind of vampire, if you know what I mean."

To demonstrate, Zander gave a leering grin. Two of his teeth grew, like magic, lengthening into pointed fangs.

Ben shivered at the sight, even though he knew he was safe.

"And that little match girl." The vampire paused while his fangs receded. "I could have helped her. That's the kind of work we VAMPs do. If only I'd known."

His voice broke as tears trickled down his sunken cheeks.

"I'm sorry I upset you," Ben said. "But when you asked me to *show* you Christmas, all I could think of were the videos."

Zander raised a tear-streaked face. "And that

Grinch who stole Christmas. Why, I'd track him to the North Pole and back. Biting *his* neck would've brought me great pleasure."

"They're only stories," Ben said, concerned at how seriously Zander was taking all this. "Don't you have stories in Multiveinia?"

"Well, of course we do. I suppose *our* stories would make *you* cry. I remember one in particular that tore me up when I read it at the tender age of 110. *Lost Feast*. The victim — a young girl who stayed too long at the fair — escaped seconds before the brave hero sampled her neck."

"Ewww," Ben said, wrinkling his nose.

Zander gave Ben a sheepish look. "Well, I guess you wouldn't feel sorry for a hero who didn't get to murder anyone. Never mind."

"Look," Ben said. "I don't have much time. Mom and I are getting a Christmas tree tonight, and — "

"A Christmas tree? Like the ones in the videos?"

"Yeah. We decorate it, then put presents underneath. It's sort of, um, a symbol of giving."

"Sounds marvelous. May I watch?"

Ben pictured himself introducing the vampire to Mom, then asking permission for Zander to join in trimming the tree. "Gee, I don't think that would be a good idea."

The vampire's face turned all blotchy, as if he

was about to start sobbing again. "What if I shape-change into smoke and sit above the fireplace to watch? Your mother won't know I'm there. Nor will you."

"Seriously?" *This is too weird.*

"Seriously."

Ben sighed. "Okay — I guess." The idea made him nervous, adding to his feelings of sadness over trimming the tree without his dad. *Oh, well. At least Dad will be home Friday to hear me sing in the Christmas program.*

"Is something amiss?" Zander asked at Ben's silence.

"It's just — " Ben stopped and shrugged. "My dad was supposed to be home tonight."

"Oh." Zander's expression turned as melancholy as Ben felt.

He wondered if talking about Dad reminded Zander that the twins still waited for his return to Multiveinia.

The vampire rested his feet on a box. His shoes seemed as long as snowboards. "Why does your father travel so much?"

"It's his job. He's a comic."

"A comic?"

"Yeah, he travels to comedy clubs and tells jokes to audiences."

"You mean, like a court jester?"

"Well, yeah. Only he doesn't wear tights, or

35

slippers with curled toes, or hats with hanging bells."

The vampire stood and stepped a few feet away. "Pretend I'm an audience, and tell me some of your father's jokes."

"Really?"

Zander adjusted his gloves. "I've been known to appreciate a good sense of humor. Count Dracula was a riot. Until he got mad, of course, and you *never* wanted to make him mad."

"You knew Count Dracula?"

"Why, yes. Who didn't? But enough about him. Tell me a joke."

Ben thought hard. Sometimes Dad tried out new material on him, but he couldn't remember any of the new stuff on demand.

"Okay," he finally said. "Here's one. When we moved to this house, we had a squirrel problem here in the attic, so my dad said to me, 'Do you know how to catch a squirrel?' I said, 'No,' so *he* said, 'Just go up to the attic and act like a nut.' "

The vampire's expression didn't change.

"That's the joke. Get it?"

"Mmmm, no. Tell me another."

Ben sighed. He'd thought that joke was hilarious the first time he heard it. Maybe he didn't tell it right. "Okay, here's one he uses in his act. And it's about *me*. He says, 'My son beats me up every morning.' Then he stops and waits for the audience to react, then says, 'My son gets up at six o'clock and I get up at seven.' "

Ben waited.

The vampire gave him an empty stare.

"Get it? I beat him up? Every morning?"

"Mmmm, no. Tell me another."

"Ben! Time to eat!" came his mother's voice.

"Gotta go. Sorry." Ben hustled toward the stairs, glad to be spared. Nothing was more unnerving than telling a joke and not getting a chuckle in return. "Guess I'll see you tomorrow."

"Wrong," the vampire said with a flip of his cape. "I'll see you tonight. You and your Christmas tree."

6.
Deck the Halls with Boughs of Horror

Borrowing Dad's truck, Ben and his mom headed down snow-packed roads toward town. The night was frigid cold, but clear. No moon shone, making the stars glow as white as vampire fangs. *Ha.* Ben laughed at the metaphor that never would've occurred to him a few days ago.

They found the perfect tree in a lot next to the Woodrock Café. The family room in their new house had a twelve-foot ceiling, so the bushy Douglas fir would be the biggest Christmas tree in Garcia family history. Ben helped tie it down in the back of the truck for the trip home.

"Who's that waiting on the porch?" Mom asked as the truck turned down Meadow Lane, slip-sliding on a patch of ice.

Ben gulped before peering toward the house. Huddled in the green-and-blue glow of Christmas lights strung across the porch was a lone figure.

He hoped it wasn't Zander, shape-changed into a door-to-door salesman.

But it wasn't the vampire. It was Thorn. A green-and-blue Thorn.

"H-i-i-i!" she called as they climbed from the truck. "My mom sent me over with a fruitcake."

Ben wanted to say, "I see *two* fruitcakes," but why give Mom an opportunity to bawl him out in front of Thorn?

"How nice, Marly," Mom called. "Won't you come in?"

Ben groaned, but not loud enough for his mother to hear.

Ignoring Thorn, he made his way through snowdrifts to the back of the truck and untied the rope. The tree was so huge, it took all three of them to get it inside the house, which almost made Ben grateful that Thorn was there. Almost.

Getting the tree upright in the stand was difficult. The floorboards in the family room were uneven, so no matter where they set the tree, it leaned. Not much, but enough to make everyone tilt their heads when they looked at it.

Mom chitchatted with Thorn as they unwrapped the fruitcake. "Marly is going to stay and help us decorate the tree," she told Ben.

Thorn smiled at him, giving a quick wave. It was the trendy "pageant wave" all the sixth-grade girls were now into.

He wrinkled his lip at her. *How could Mom invite a stranger to join our night of family tradition?*

You invited a stranger, too. Actually, he invited himself.

I forgot! Ben's gaze darted around the room. "Can I build a fire?" he asked. Might seem strange to see smoke floating above the fireplace without a roaring fire beneath it.

"Sure," Mom answered. "Marly, why don't you pick out some Christmas music to put us in the tree-trimming spirit while I call your mom and tell her you're staying."

They attended to their separate chores. Mom brought in a pitcher of eggnog and a tin of cookies, then opened the ornament boxes. Every year, she became more and more finicky about decorating the tree "her way," as if each ornament must be hung in a certain order and a certain place.

"Marly, you work from this box. Ben, here's yours. We'll save the family heirloom ornaments for last."

Ben moved his box to the opposite side of the room from Thorn. He glanced at the smoke rising above the flames. Was Zander there? Was he enjoying himself? Or was he crying again? Could puffs of smoke cry?

"I smell smoke," Marly said. "I mean, over here by the tree."

Mom rushed to check the string of lights, making sure none of the cords had been damaged when they moved. "Mmmm," she said. "I smell smoke, too. I'll have Mildred check the wiring in this room, just to be safe."

She crawled under the tree to look over the rest of the lights. "Ben, did you remember to open the damper in the fireplace?"

Yes, he'd remembered, but he checked anyway to please her. He knew why they smelled smoke on the wrong side of the room. Zander.

"That's odd," his mother added.

Ben gulped. *Odd* was not a word he wanted to hear tonight. "What's odd?"

"Well . . ." She paused, surveying the room as though someone else were there, hiding behind the sofa or crouching behind an end table.

Ben didn't like the curious expression on her face.

"We always save the heirloom ornaments for last, but three of them are missing. And look. There they are, already on the tree."

"I didn't touch them!" Marly blurted.

"I know you didn't, dear." She eyed Ben. "Did you put them on?"

"Mmmm." He wasn't good at fibbing. He always got caught. "I must have," he fibbed. *Zander, are you doing this?* How could a wisp of smoke decorate a tree?

41

Mom frowned at him, rearranging the ornaments *her* way. She fetched a ladder from the pantry and climbed up to place the Christmas angel on top of the tree. Ben's grandmother had made the angel, dressing her in a flowing white robe and gold-sprinkled mesh wings.

"Oh, it's beautiful, Mrs. Garcia," Marly said. "Isn't it, Ben?"

Before Ben could answer, a movement caught his eye. A silver star — from the heirloom box — floated across the room by itself. Well, not exactly by itself. A puff of smoke surrounded it.

In two steps, Ben was there, pretending to hold it while it floated.

"Be-en! Why are you hanging *those* before you've finished with your own? Didn't I — ?"

"Does it really matter what order we put these on?" He stepped back to his assigned box, exasperated at her *and* at Zander. And Thorn, too, simply for being there.

Mom stared down at him, much like the Christmas angel. "Yeah, it matters," she told him. "Just do it to humor me, okay?"

Why'd she have to be so persnickety? He hoped Zander had heard his mother's words and stopped fooling around. Hadn't the vampire promised no one would know he was there?

Marly laughed at him, which made Ben angry

for getting into trouble because of the vampire.

Suddenly, a glittery-red bell rose from the box and floated across the room. *Zander!* Ben yelled in his mind. *Stop it!*

Rushing to intercept, he tried to lead the bell back to its box. Thorn was gaping at him, as if she couldn't believe he'd done it again.

So was his mother. "Benjamin Avery, why are you disobey — ?"

The doorbell rang. Marly clicked off the music. Voices outside were singing "Joy to the World."

Ben breathed a sigh of relief. *Saved by the bell.*

Mom hopped off the ladder and rushed into the entry hall. Opening the door, she greeted the neighbors and townspeople who'd come caroling. The group was bundled in so many layers against the cold night air, they more or less waddled into the entry hall like a flock of penguins.

Ben stepped to the doorway and listened to the singing. Marly squeezed next to him as the group launched into "Here We Come a' Caroling." He hoped none of the visitors noticed the areas of missing wallpaper in the entry hall, or the worn carpet. Having company before Mom finished remodeling the house embarrassed him.

Too nervous to stand still, he worked his way backward into the family room so he could keep one eye on the tree.

Marly followed.

Why does she have to be here, complicating everything?

"What are you doing?" she asked.

"Nothing." The instant he said it, his eyes were drawn to a green shepherd's staff rising over Thorn's head.

"Thorn!" he blurted, twirling her around so her back was to the tree.

She jumped, giggling at him. "What?"

"Um, let's sing with the carolers," was the only plan he could come up with to distract her.

Behind Marly, the remaining ornaments floated to the tree in rapid succession. Next, tinsel sprinkled down upon the branches like silver rain. Then, the Christmas angel pivoted with a jerk, facing the center of the room.

Horror filled Ben's chest. What if someone noticed? They'd think the house was haunted. His mom would freak and move out. Then he'd have to change schools again. Didn't Zander realize how dangerous this was?

Meanwhile, he was forced to stand there singing "Up on the Housetop" while acting as though he was having a wonderful time.

After a solemn rendering of "Hark the Herald Angels Sing," Mom offered dessert to the carolers. Ben hoped they'd take all of Thorn's fruitcake so he didn't have to eat any of it.

After everyone left, Mom hurried back to the family room, acting eager to resume her role as Director of Tree Trimming. "Ben!" she cried. "You finished by yourself." Her voice sounded upset instead of pleased.

Ben shrugged.

Marly stared at the tree. "How did you — ?"

"It was nothing," he said before she could finish her question.

"But I like the angel facing the other direction," Mom told him. "Put it back the way I had it. Then please walk Marly home; it's getting late."

Mith, Ben swore to himself. Climbing the ladder, his eyes shifted one way, then the other. Scanning the room for a puff of smoke wasn't easy. He rotated the angel and climbed down.

Throwing on his coat, he *ran* Thorn home instead of *walking* her there, in spite of her pleas to slow down. But his pace kept her from demanding to know how the tree decorated itself while they sang Christmas carols.

Back at home, he and Mom sprawled on the floor in front of the fire, enjoying the music, the blinking tree lights, and the cookies.

But Ben couldn't relax. His eyes stayed on the angel, waiting for her to pivot on her own. Back to the way the vampire wanted it.

"Time for bed," Mom finally said, pulling the plug on the lights. Ben closed the fireplace doors, hoping he wasn't trapping Zander inside. As he headed off to bed, he stole one last look at the tree.

Slowly, slowly the angel turned, facing the center of the room.

7.
Fangs for
the Memories

Ben tried to stay awake until Mom went to bed so he could sneak upstairs and yell at the vampire.

But Mom was stationed at the kitchen table working on contracts for clients. The only way Ben could sneak past her was to shape-change into Licorice — which would be cool if he could do it. Finally he gave up and set his alarm an hour early.

Then he fell asleep.

Visions of sugarplums did *not* dance through his head. Visions of unearthed graves, bloody fangs, swarms of bats tangling in his hair — *that's* what danced through his head.

When the alarm buzzed, Ben felt as though he'd spent the night fleeing for his life. He could barely drag himself from bed. Night still cloaked the house, so he stumbled a lot, tiptoeing through the kitchen and pantry and up the attic stairs.

The darkness was suffocating. Especially after

47

the night he'd suffered. Every creak of the floor-boards blanketed him with dread.

Ben clicked on the attic light. One, to prevent more stumbling in the dark, and two, it would be the quickest way to get the vampire's attention.

The attic was quiet and freezing cold. More snow had fallen during the night, and, in his haste, Ben had left his robe and slippers behind.

He stood on one foot, then the other, trying to warm them against his pajama legs. Where was Zander? Why wasn't he fussing over the light?

Ben marched toward the vampire's corner, keeping one eye on the rafters. Was the attic's resident in bat form? If so, what if he took on the mentality of a bat? Was there such a thing as a polite bat with manners? One who wouldn't dream of tangling in your hair? Or sucking your blood?

Ben shuddered, searching the rafters until his neck hurt. He didn't like fluttery things.

The vampire wasn't here — as a bat or himself.

Sitting on a box to wait, Ben curled his feet under his legs to keep them warm. All the anger he'd harbored for the vampire faded with time. Neither Mom nor Thorn had figured out that something supernatural was going on last night, yet the evening was horrible when it was supposed to be special. Didn't that justify a little anger?

The vampire's belongings were scattered about. Strung in the corner was a crystal sleigh adorned with faded ribbons, a bread-dough reindeer, and a tinfoil candy cane Ben had made in first grade.

"Zander, you snitched Mom's ornaments!"

Underneath, a fat evergreen branch sat propped in a vase. Cobwebs graced the branches like angel wings. A pine cone Santa, another of Ben's early creations, was clipped to the top.

"Oh, great," Ben muttered, recognizing the vase. "Now he's unpacking our boxes." He touched the branch. "Where did this come from? The backyard? The tree downstairs?" Ben imagined a gaping hole in front of the Christmas tree. "Oh, please, no."

He kicked at one of the boxes, hurting his bare toe. "Zander, you're blowing it. I promised to keep you a secret, but you have to cooperate. At this rate, the whole town will soon know about the Garcias' vampire. Won't *that* make me popular at school."

A leatherbound notebook lay beneath the "tree." Ben picked it up and leafed through it. Written in old English script were daily entries, memories, poems, and sketches.

Ben studied one of the drawings. A thin woman in a long dress, with lengths and lengths of dark hair, stood sandwiched in between two kids in caps and knickers. A boy and a girl. Twins. Zander Junior and Zandra. Boy, would they stick out at Rollingwood.

Ben flipped through the journal. Guilt nudged him to stop. Why was he snooping through the vampire's private possessions? His mind told him to shut the book, but his curiosity made him keep turning pages.

He stopped at an entry dated 1761:

I've found her at last. The instant I set eyes upon her, I knew she was the one I'd cherish for life. Layla, oh beautiful Layla. Your eyes turn my heart to rose petals. Your touch springs poetry from my lips. Won't you be mine? Tonight I will ask the Count for your hand in marriage.

The Count? Count Dracula? Ben closed the journal and shuddered. *Was Layla the daughter of Dracula?*

Maybe these were things he shouldn't be reading. Ben glanced toward the window. Dawn's first rays streaked pink across the eastern sky.

The family sketch and centuries-old love letter left a soft spot in Ben's heart, dissolving the rest of his anger. Unable to resist one last glance, he opened the journal again. The newest entry said:

Benjamin reminds me of my son. He's a strong, handsome lad, with much loyalty toward me. He's truly gifted with a voice as moving as Baron von Strassburg's, whom Layla and I heard perform in Vampire of the Opera at the Alpine Theatre in Vienna in 1801.

A gust of wind hit Ben's face the same moment his ears heard a noisy flapping of wings. His gaze was drawn toward the window. A dark form whooshed through the broken pane and fluttered about the attic.

As Ben watched, a mist formed, swirling like a twister. The wind died down, and there stood Zander in human form.

Ben's amazement at what he'd just observed was overshadowed by his fear of being caught snooping through the vampire's book of memories.

Would Zander be angry? Ben reminded himself that he was dealing with an undead person who'd bitten zillions of people during the last three hundred years.

His neck began to ache at the thought. Inconspicuously, he put the journal back, then, to make amends, dashed across the attic and flipped off the light.

"G-good morning," Ben said, winding his way back to Zander's corner. Why did it surprise him to know the vampire had been out during the night? Did he really think Zander stayed in the attic the whole time?

The look on the vampire's face was hard to read. Ben's plan to yell at him over last night's ornament-floating episode seemed pointless now.

"What is it?"

"I received a message in the night."

"Yeah?" Ben was so relieved that Zander didn't notice his snooping, he almost missed the quiver in the vampire's voice. "What news?"

"He's on his way."

"Who?"

"The Czar of all Vampires. King of the Undead. Emperor of Doom. The Count of Ghastly Castle."

Ben gasped. "You mean — ?"

"Yes," Zander answered in a grim voice. "The Big Guy."

8.
A Hawk and a Thorn

I hear your dad's pretty funny," came the dreaded voice of The Hawk before third period.

Ben pulled his history text from his backpack. He never told anyone what his dad did for a living. He didn't have to. The information always spread through school within months of his arrival, thanks to Dad's local TV appearances and newspaper interviews.

"So, what happened to *you*, man?" Hawk jeered, punctuating his question with a two-knuckle jab to Ben's shoulder. "You're not funny at all. As a matter of fact, you're pathetic."

"Learn a new word?" Ben was sorry the instant he said it.

Hawk's second jab surely left bruises. Ben refused to react or to rub his shoulder, which hurt like. . . . "Mith!" he blurted, not really knowing what it meant. Still it felt good to swear at Hawk in Multiveinese.

"Mith?" Hawk repeated. Then, "Hey, I just figured out what part of *funny* you inherited from your dad. Funny-*looking*." He howled at his own joke. "So when do we get to meet this hilarious father of yours, man? Is he coming to the Christmas program?"

Ben didn't answer. His mind was too busy visualizing all the calamities that might befall him at the concert.

"I asked you a question." Hawk slowly massaged his knuckles.

Ben shifted in his desk to face Hawk. His name fit him well. Beady eyes squinted above a hook nose. Dark fuzz shaded his upper lip. *How come he's growing a mustache already? He's only in the sixth grade. Did he get left back?*

"Well?" Hawk barked.

"Yeah," Ben said. "My dad's coming to the Christmas program. What's it to *you?*"

Hawk readied another two-knuckle jab. Only this one was aimed at Ben's nose.

The bell rang. Mr. Rosetti burst through the doorway. Ben and his nose were extremely grateful.

The teacher moved across the front of the room, tossing graded history reports toward the proper rows. Ben hated the way everyone looked — or snickered — at your grade, then read the teacher's comments before passing the paper back. He wished Mr. Rosetti respected his students' privacy.

Ben snatched his paper from the kid in front of him, who'd held onto it too long. D+ graced the top in blood-red. Mr. Rosetti had scribbled:

Not your usual conscientious work, Mr. Garcia. Getting too caught up in the Christmas spirit?

"Right," Ben muttered, shoving the report into his backpack before Hawk could comment on the grade. He settled in as Mr. Rosetti launched into a lecture on the creation of the Senate and the House of Representatives.

Ben zoned out. He had more important things to think about. *What would Mr. Rosetti say if I raised my hand to tell the class that the Emperor of Doom is on his way to Woodrock?*

The bizarreness struck Ben funny. He swallowed a chuckle knowing Mr. Rosetti would be insulted if someone laughed in the middle of his lecture. Nothing about the House or the Senate was funny.

Ben thought back to his conversation with Zander. The big question was — how did he receive the message that The Big Guy was coming?

Zander's answer seemed so simple: "The same way I get my assignments and my catalog orders of herbal blood. They come on a cloud or a breeze, by owl or viper, by whisper from a mist, or by shout from a hurricane."

"Oh," Ben had said, for lack of a better answer. What had he expected the vampire to tell him? By Federal Express?

"Hi-i-i-i, Be-e-en."

Marly Thorn slid into the seat next to him in music class. He hated the way she dragged out her hellos. It reminded him of the way mothers addressed their two-year-olds.

"Hi," he answered. She wore Christmas bells in her hair, on her red sweater, and on her socks. Every time she moved, she jingled.

"Are you ready for the big night?" Jingle, jingle.

He shrugged. *Yikes. How can I concentrate on my solo when the King of the Undead is on his way to my house?* The thought made his blood step on the brakes. *Please, Big Guy, don't show up tomorrow night.*

"Ben? Are you okay?" Marly wiggled his arm, as if trying to wake him.

He realized he'd been gazing out the window, hypnotized by the falling snow. "I'm fine. Why?" Suddenly he didn't know whether he'd *thought* "King of the Undead" or said it out loud.

"Well, your face got real pale all of a sudden."

Not knowing what to answer, he said nothing.

56

Thankfully, Ms. Sasaki bounded into the room, allowing him to forget about the Thorn at his side. Ha. He laughed at his own cleverness.

"This is it, people," the teacher said. "Our last practice. Tomorrow is show time."

Some cheered; some groaned, depending on how ready they were, or how nervous they'd become about singing in front of their families.

The practice went well. Everyone made it through the Daffy Duck song without stumbling. The better they sounded, the harder they tried. Ben could tell by Ms. Sasaki's grin that she was pleased — for a change.

The dulcimer intro to his solo played. He felt good, confident. Taking a deep breath, he closed his eyes to concentrate on hitting the right notes. Then he began.

He got as far as "Long lay the world in sin and error pining" before he heard the groans and laughter, and realized that the music had stopped.

Ben opened his eyes. Everyone was watching him, *glaring* at him, saying things like "Way to go, Garcia" in sarcastic voices.

"Huh?" He looked to the teacher for support. "What did I do?" *Was I off-key? Did I miss my cue?* he added to himself.

"Are you all right?" Ms. Sasaki asked.

"I'm fine." *Why does everyone keep asking if I'm all right?*

"Why did you do it?" She hopped off the chair to restart the music.

"Do what?"

More groans. More laughter.

"Ben Garcia," she said, sounding incredulous. "Aren't you aware of the fact that you just ruined our program by singing, 'Oh holy bite, the Czar is nightly dining'?"

9.
Reverse the Curse

Ben didn't say much the rest of the day, or on the bus. Kids kept pointing at him, whisper-laughing, and shaking their heads. Even Marly Thorn seemed too embarrassed to sit next to him. She jingled right past, sitting in back with the eighth-graders.

He didn't feel much like talking when he got home, either, but he still had a zillion unanswered questions for Zander.

Ben trudged up the porch steps, stopping to adjust a string of lights. He was bummed to-day, anyway, because he and his dad were sup-posed to go Christmas shopping tonight. Oh, well. One more day and Dad would be home for the holidays.

His mother was in the kitchen, sanding layers of paint off the trim on the cabinet doors while waiting for a cake to bake. He'd hoped to beat her home so he wouldn't need an excuse for a trip to the attic.

"Baking for the church again?" Ben teased, wishing she baked sometimes just for him.

"This time, it's for school. Ms. Sasaki called to see if I'd contribute refreshments for the Christmas program."

"She did?"

Mom gave him a concerned look. Sawdust sprinkled the top of her head like snowflakes.

Uh-oh. Did Ms. Sasaki tell her what happened today?

"Your teacher asked me if everything was okay here at home, and if you'd been displaying any changes in behavior. Those were her words, by the way." Mom watched his face, motioning toward a spatula she'd saved for him to lick. "Honey, is something bothering you?"

"No." He slurped chocolate from the spatula. "Nothing at all."

She gave him her worried-mother look, the way she did when he was sick with the flu.

"Honest, Mom. Everything's fine." How could he warn her what might happen in the next few days when he didn't know himself? It was on his list of questions for Zander.

"Okay. Just remember, you can always tell me if something is wrong."

"I know." Ben felt a tug toward the attic stairs,

almost as if Zander were invisibly pulling on him. "Can I go now?"

"One more question."

He stopped.

"I seem to be missing some Christmas ornaments. I swear I saw them on the tree last night, but now they're gone."

She gave the wood trim a few more strokes with the sandpaper. "I must be imagining things, but it's been so hectic with Christmas shopping, fixing up the house, and dealing with clients in a hurry to sign final papers so they can move over the holiday."

Rinsing her hands, she checked on the cake. "Would you scout around for the ornaments? A few belonged to my grandmother, so I want to give them their rightful place on the tree."

"I'll look in the attic," Ben offered. "There are still lots of boxes up there." *Brilliant*, he added to himself.

"Great. Oh, and one more thing. Will you *please* quit turning the Christmas angel toward the center of the room? I put it the way I want, but the next time I walk past, it's turned the other way." She planted a kiss on his forehead. "Isn't it a bit close to Christmas for you to be so ornery? Or is our new house haunted?"

Ben's grin faded. So Zander was zipping around the house while he was at school. He hoped the vampire disguised his movements. The thought of him coming face to face with Mom was not something Ben wanted to add to his list of worries.

Shoving the spatula into the dishwasher, he hustled to the attic.

"What took you so long?" Zander hissed the instant Ben hit the top step. "Your bus went by a half hour ago."

"How'd *you* know? You can't look out the window; it's still daylight."

"Yes! That's what I've been *dying* to tell you — if you'll pardon the pun." The vampire grabbed Ben's arm. They were instantly at a front window. Ben was certain he hadn't walked there. *How'd Zander do that?*

"Look!" The vampire threw open the shutter, letting afternoon light spill into the room. It wasn't all that bright because snow was still falling, yet daylight was daylight. Zander didn't even flinch.

"What does this mean?" Ben had no idea.

"It means, that after a decade of not drinking real blood, my body seems to be adapting to things all vampires detest. I'm not thrilled with the light, mind you, but I can tolerate it. And look . . ."

Zander grabbed Ben's arm again. They were instantly in his corner. How they got there, Ben wasn't sure. "Do you know what this is?" Zander held up a bottle that greatly resembled one from Mom's spice rack.

"Garlic?" Ben exclaimed. "You're holding a jar of garlic?"

"Yes! It's not something I'd wear around my neck, but I can be close to it, and it doesn't send me flying in the other direction."

Ben was amazed.

"Look at this." Zander flung open the shutter in his corner. Beyond the dirty window lay the forest. "I went for a stroll in those trees this afternoon. It was lovely, and much dimmer in there than out in the meadow. I'm going back tomorrow."

Suddenly he grew misty-eyed. "I only wish I could show Layla, but with HIM after me, I've only a matter of days, perhaps hours until . . ."

While he waited for the vampire to regain his composure, the "big picture" began to form in Ben's mind. "Stop crying," he said. "I have a plan."

"Indeed? Oh, I *do* so love it when *somebody* has a plan."

"Sit," Ben ordered. It was easier to talk to the vampire while he was sitting. The gap in their heights wasn't as noticeable.

Zander sat.

"Your family is in Multiveinia, right?"

He nodded.

"Can you send for them? As in sending a message on a breeze or by owl? The way you told me?"

"Send for them to come *here?* Why, they've never gone on assignment with me. They can't. It's a Big Guy law."

"You're not *on* assignment anymore, and you've already broken The Big Guy's law."

"Oh, right." Zander pulled off a glove and began to bite his nails. His gaze shifted around the attic, which made Ben feel like biting his own nails.

"He isn't here yet, is he?" Ben asked.

"No, but I heard — from the sunrise — that he's taking care of other matters on his way. I only hope his other matters don't involve my V.A.M.P. colleagues."

"What if, when The Big Guy gets here, he can't touch you?"

"Because . . . ?" Zander said, encouraging Ben to continue.

"Because you've managed to reverse the curse."

"Reverse the curse," Zander repeated, eyes sparking life for the very first time. "Reverse the curse, reverse the curse, REVERSE THE CURSE!"

He danced around his corner, singing the words. "I like it," he said at the end of his dance. "But how? How do we reverse the curse?"

Ben sighed. It was tough coming up with all the answers. Especially answers he wasn't quite sure of. "I don't know. But if The Big Guy has power over you because of the vampire curse, yet you're becoming *immune* to the curse, his hold might not be as strong."

Zander gave a thoughtful "Mmmm."

"I need to know the whole story," Ben finished. "How you became a vampire, and all that. What The Big Guy might do to you. I think we can stand up to him. Or, at least *you* can," Ben added quickly. Not much *he* could do, being human and all. *Gulp.*

"Ben, what's taking you so long?" came his mom's voice. "Dinner's ready; get down here."

Ben snatched his mother's ornaments from Zander's corner. "I'll try to come back tonight after Mom goes to bed."

"No," Zander said, gazing longingly at the ornaments. "Too risky. I'll come to you."

"Benjamin Avery Garcia!"

Zander took hold of Ben's arm and pinched it. When he let go, Ben was taking the last step from the pantry into the kitchen.

10.
The Seventh Son

Ben slouched at his desk during English, listening to the last few oral reports before Christmas break.

Zander didn't come last night. Ben had stayed awake, waiting for a twister to appear at the foot of his bed, a wisp of smoke to whoosh under the door, or a bat to attach itself to the window screen.

Nothing happened. Nothing except major nightmares, as vivid as a video. That, and the solution to Zander's dilemma.

The solution had come before he'd fallen asleep. This morning, it danced outside of his consciousness. He knew it was a good idea, but he couldn't pin it down. It kept fluttering from his grasp, like the moths he used to chase in the springtime.

Yet, something made him empty his life's savings from the shoe box under his bed — if $27.31 can be considered a life's savings.

It wasn't until Marly Thorn got up to give her

oral report on "The True Meaning of Christmas" that Ben's idea lunged from the shadowed corners of his brain and took a bow in the spotlight.

He jerked up straight in his desk. "Yes, yes!" he blurted, right in the middle of Marly's talk.

Marly must have thought her smarmy speech had moved him, so she jingled down his aisle and delivered the rest of her talk practically in his lap.

The true meaning of Christmas. Reverse the curse. That's it!

He could hardly wait to tell Zander.

As soon as English was over, Ben hurried straight to the gym, where student council officers were sponsoring the "Elf Bazaar." They wore tights and baggy shirts, belted in the middle, with Santa caps and fake beards. Even the girls.

Tons of gifts, new and almost-new, donated by the student body were scattered out on tables. Every gift cost one dollar. For an extra quarter, an elf gift-wrapped it in recycled paper of holly-berry-red and mistletoe green in assorted designs.

A half hour later, Ben's backpack was filled with twenty-one wrapped gifts — and a dollar with change left for his life's savings' shoe box.

He couldn't wait for the final bell. Students were bouncing off the walls. They always did the last day before holiday break, but kids from the choir were worse. Opening-night jitters, Ben guessed. He hoped they calmed down before tonight. He hoped *he* calmed down before tonight.

He beat his mother home, which thrilled him immensely. Now he could talk to Zander without making up excuses for being in the attic.

Ben practically crashed through the door at the top of the stairs. "Where were you last night?" he huffed, relieved to find the vampire there instead of taking his afternoon stroll through the forest.

Zander looked up from where he sat writing in his journal.

The sight twinged Ben with guilt, especially since he'd read the entry that said, "Benjamin reminds me of my son. He's a strong, handsome lad, with much loyalty to me. . . ."

"I was in you room," Zander said, closing the journal.

Ben scrunched his face. "What do you mean? I didn't see you."

"No, but you dreamed about me, didn't you?"

"Yes." How could he forget? The dreams were so vivid, he . . .

Zander grinned, but refrained from sliding his fangs into place.

"Was my dream true? Did all those things really happen?"

The vampire nodded.

"You mean," Ben began, reluctant to recall the dream that gave him nightmares. "You were bound to live in Ghastly Castle when you came of age? You were trained by The Big Guy's evil servants? And the day a visiting count arrived with his daughter, you, you bit her neck and turned her into a vampire, too, and — "

"Well, I wasn't too proud of that part, but . . . in the end, Layla fell in love with my charming ways and forgave me. She agreed to be my wife, and really, we've been blissfully happy these past two hundred years. She's quite content now to be immortal."

Ben closed his eyes to recall the beginning of the dream. "I still don't know how you *became* a vampire. Did The Big Guy bite you? Or did someone else?"

He pulled up the nearest box and sat, waiting to hear what he hoped to be a gross and gruesome story.

The vampire absently brushed lint off his cape. "I always skim over that part. It's really a nonstory. I never had a chance to be a real human being. I was born the seventh son of a seventh son, which carries the curse from beyond the beginning of time."

"You were *born* with the curse?"

Zander nodded, looking sad. "My dear mother

had hoped not to have more than six lads. But, alas, I arrived. I do have fond memories of my early life, though — playing with my brothers. Mother baking her wonderful apple strudel with vanilla sauce. Mmmm, I can almost smell it cooling on the hearth."

Ben was fascinated with Zander's life story, yet there wasn't time to reminisce. Mom would be home soon, bringing his dad from the airport. They'd barely have time to eat before the Christmas program. His stomach lurched at the thought. Maybe he'd skip dinner.

"So," Ben said, interrupting the vampire's memories. "Moving to Ghastly Castle was part of the curse?"

"Yes. The seventh son was given over to the Czar, the King, the Emperor — "

"The Count, The Big Guy," Ben finished. "The one who's coming for Christmas."

He said it in jest, but his own words shivered chills through him.

A distant ringing snapped him back to this century. "The phone!" He dashed downstairs to the kitchen. Zander followed.

A moment later, Ben hung up, unable to face the vampire because he felt tears on the horizon and he didn't want to cry in front of anyone.

"Benjamin?" Zander's voice was soft. "What's wrong?"

He tried to explain, but his words stepped on each others' toes instead of lining up to exit his mouth in the proper order.

"Son, what is it? Tell me."

Hearing Zander call him *son* didn't help. "My dad," he said in a voice two octaves higher than his speaking voice.

"He's *dead?!*" Zander cried. "Oh merciful mith!"

"No." Ben laughed at the shocked look on Zander's face. "He's not dead. He's snowed in. No flights are leaving Altoona. He won't be here in time to hear me sing."

"Oh-h-h." Zander actually hugged him. Somehow the hug made Ben feel a whole lot better — in spite of its icy coldness.

"Mom will make it to the program, but she told me to call the Thorns for a ride." The last thing Ben wanted was to ride to the program with Miss Jingle Bells.

"Thorn," Zander repeated. "Thorn and Hawk."

"What? How did you — ?"

"After I sent my dream, you fell into one of your own. One that greatly troubled you. It concerned a thorn and a hawk."

"You can read my dreams?"

"Not usually, but it rode the coattails of *my* dream, so I was able to absorb it."

"Wow." Quickly Ben filled Zander in on his

Thorn and Hawk problem, while attempting to eat a bowl of cornflakes for dinner. They mostly caught in his throat, but managed to squelch his hunger.

"Well," he said when finished. "I guess it's time to call the Thorns."

Zander was thoughtful. "I have a plan."

His words reminded Ben that he'd forgotten to tell Zander his great idea. "Oh, *you* have a plan this time," he teased. "That's refreshing." He chuckled, more from the unbelievable sight of a vampire sitting at the kitchen table than from his teasing.

Zander gave him a serious look. "*I* will take you to the program."

Ben was confused. "Do you drive?"

"No. But we'll get there. Trust me."

"Oh." Ben remembered the way Zander zipped him around the attic. "Cool. *Then* what? You drop me off and come home?"

Zander leaned back in his chair, acting offended. "My dear Benjamin, I wouldn't miss hearing you sing for all the black capes in Multiveinia."

Ben remembered his dad saying the same thing. Except for the black capes and Multiveinia part. "You'll stay at school? Where will you hide?"

"Why do I have to hide?"

"I think the answer is obvious."

"Dear boy, if it's your desire to go to the program tonight with your father, you will." He stood and bowed his elegant bow. "*I* will attend as your father."

11.
Hark! The Comic Vampire Comes

Standing in the kitchen one moment, then stepping into the school auditorium the next was so cool, Ben wished he could do it all the time. Only he could think of better destinations — like Disney World.

The second they materialized at school, Ben whisked Zander backstage. Dressing him in Dad's clothes had seemed a great idea at first. Unfortunately, Dad was not seven feet tall. The Dockers hit Zander mid-calf; the sweater sleeves came to his elbows.

Ben thought Dad's plaid raincoat might cover the ill-fitting clothes, but the coat fell way above Zander's knees. The effect was pretty ludicrous.

At first, Ben thought Zander planned to *shape-change* into Dad, but then he explained that vampires can shape-change into animals and various other things — but not people.

At least the vampire had agreed to watch the concert from backstage instead of sitting in the audience next to Ben's mom. His decision brought great relief to Ben, who was sure he'd panic from the risers if he saw the two chitchatting.

Backstage, Ben steered Zander into the folds of the curtain, trying to make him as inconspicuous as possible. Kids were already giving him double takes. "Stand here and don't move or speak to anyone," Ben told him. "The second I finish my solo, go home. Mom will drive me back."

"Why, Ben, this must be your father."

Ben gulped before turning to greet Ms. Sasaki, who barely came up to the vampire's waist. She wore a glittery red dress with red satin heels. Ben thought she and Zander looked like Beauty and the Beast.

"Um, Zan, I mean, *Dad*, this is my music teacher."

The vampire gave one of his impressive bows, taking Ms. Sasaki's hand and kissing it. "I am truly charmed to meet you, miss."

"Oh!" the teacher exclaimed.

"Oh, what?" blurted Ben. Did Zander nibble on her hand?

"My goodness, you're ice-cold," she said. "I'll go turn up the heat." She left in a flurry of red.

Ben chuckled. Turning up the heat was *not* going to warm up *this* guy.

"So, you're the famous Mr. Garcia."

The voice made Ben cringe.

Hawk gave Zander a once-over, snickering. "New stage costume?"

The vampire studied Hawk, as if trying to place where he'd seen him before. "And you are?"

How could Zander be so polite? "This is *Hawk*," Ben said, putting emphasis on the name.

"Ah, Mr. Hawk. Pleased to make your acquaintance."

"Say something funny, man."

Zander looked confused. "I beg your pardon?"

"Tell me some jokes; you must have a million of 'em." Hawk raised on his tiptoes to make himself appear taller. "So, make me laugh."

Ms. Sasaki rustled past again, stopping when she heard Hawk's comment. "Yes, I read an article about you. Do tell us one of your jokes."

Ben panicked. His deception was about to be exposed. "Um, Dad just got home from a trip. He's too tired to — "

"No, son, it's quite all right. I don't mind doing a little entertaining. I *am* standing on a stage, aren't I? Ah, ha, ha, ha."

Oh, no, here it comes.

"Ha   ha   ha!"
    ha   ha   ha   ha
       ha   ha   ha   ha
          ha   ha

Hawk and Ms. Sasaki took three steps backward. Their eyebrows seemed painted in the "surprised" position.

"Did we miss something?" Hawk scoffed. "Like, the joke?"

Zander regained his composure. "Here are some jokes from my act." He cleared his throat. "Do you know how to catch a squirrel?"

They shook their heads. Ms. Sasaki smiled in anticipation of the punch line.

Ben groaned, yet the vampire's quick thinking impressed him.

"You catch a squirrel by going to the attic and acting . . . goofy!

"Ha   ha   ha!"
    ha   ha   ha   ha
       ha   ha   ha   ha
          ha   ha

They stared at Zander. Other kids stopped to join the staring.

Ben wished he could pinch his own arm for an

77

instant trip home to his bedroom. Once there, he'd stay for a decade or two.

Zander gulped a few times, catching his breath. "Here's another one."

NO! Ben screamed in his mind.

"Do you know why," the vampire began, "I beat my son up every morning?"

Ben cringed.

Ms. Sasaki's smile faded. "Really, Mr. Garcia, jokes like that are *not* welcome. Child abuse is a terrible problem." She turned, shooting Ben a sympathetic look before stalking off.

Ben stalked off in the opposite direction. *Thanks a lot, Zan.*

"No. Why do you beat your son up every morning?"

Hawk! Ben whipped around to listen. Was it possible for the vampire to slaughter the joke any more than he already had?

"Because I have to get up early."

Hawk waited for the rest of the punch line, but Zander was silent, grinning from pointed ear to pointed ear.

"That's it?" he jeered. "You beat your son because you have to get up early?"

"Yes!" Zander beamed at Ben, looking quite pleased with himself.

"Show time!" called Marly Thorn.

For once, Ben was glad for Thorn's interruption.

Instantly, the stage came to life as white-robed choir members scrambled for their spots on the risers. Someone pulled the heavy curtain, blocking everyone's view of the crowded auditorium.

Above the risers, yellow stars sprinkled with glitter hung from strings tied to the lights. A background scene, painted on cardboard, sat propped on ladders behind the risers so it could be seen over all the heads.

The scene depicted a sleigh, pulled by chestnut horses, heading toward a cozy-looking church in the distance. Smoke curled from the chimney, and villagers, bundled in long capes, waved to one other.

Ben fidgeted on the third step of the risers. Wearing a robe under the hot lights was uncomfortable. He tried to pretend it was a vampire cape, even though it was white instead of black. But it didn't work. Right now, he was pretty disgusted with the only vampire in his life.

He yanked at the tight collar pinching his neck. How could he hit the high notes when he could hardly breathe?

"What happened to *you?*" Marly Thorn jingled to her place on the risers. She'd added more bells to her hair, and pinned a few onto her robe. "You were supposed to ride to school with us tonight."

"I, um, got a ride with my dad." Ben bit his tongue. Fudging this close to Christmas broke one of the basic rules of his life.

"I thought your father was stranded at some airport."

"No, he's here." *Please don't ask to meet him.*

"But your mom's sitting alone."

"Well, Dad's backstage," Ben explained, pointing in the general direction. "He's, uh, used to being onstage, you know."

"Do you need a ride home?" Marly smiled, tilting her head. Jingle, jingle, went her bells.

"No thank you." Ben was polite to make up for his earlier fudging.

"Places, everyone!" called Ms. Sasaki, smiling right at Ben. "It's time."

She feels sorry for me now. Ben sighed. *I will do my best. I will sing better than I've ever sung in my life. Just for you, Ms. Sasaki.*

The rustling of robes stopped. The teacher put two fingers to her lips — her signal to the choir to refrain from talking while she greeted the audience.

Leaving the choir at attention, she slipped through the curtain.

Applause filled the air. Then Ms. Sasaki told the parents how hard their sons and daughters had worked to prepare for the Christmas program, and how proud she was of each and every one of them. Especially her lead vocalist, Benjamin Garcia.

A round of sarcastic "O-o-o-o-o"s made Ben wish she hadn't singled him out. This could increase his torment for the rest of the year.

"Teacher's pet, huh?" came Hawk's voice. "We'll see."

Ben yanked at his collar. *I'm doomed, doomed, doomed.*

The curtain parted, lights dimmed, music began. Ms. Sasaki looked like a Christmas ornament posed on top of a box she'd covered with red foil.

"It's Beginning to Look a Lot Like Christmas" started with a wobble or two, but smoothed out as kids calmed down. This was just like practice in the choir room. Only two hundred or so people watched and listened.

A few kids gave in to giggle attacks during the Daffy Duck song, tangling their tongues over "Thou Doth Watcheth Over Thee."

Ben ignored them, working hard to stay focused. So far, he'd been singing great. Hitting every note and cue. *Stay focused,* he repeated to himself. *My solo will sound better than it ever has. Ms. Sasaki won't be sorry she told the audience how hard I've worked.*

Ben listened to the dulcimer chime the intro to

his song. He glued his gaze onto Ms. Sasaki's right hand so he wouldn't miss her cue. *Stay focused. Clear your throat. Get ready. Take a breath. Go.*

"O holy night, the stars are brightly shining . . ."

Yes! His voice was strong and clear. *Perfect!*

Ms. Sasaki beamed at him. His mom wiped a tear from her cheek. *Stay focused.*

"For yonder breaks a new and glorious morn."

Something was wrong. Someone was humming in his ear. A different song than Ben was singing. A song with a faster beat.

Hawk!

Ben panicked. His heart pounded like the kettledrums in "We Three Kings." His voice lost strength, going breathy on him. He couldn't maintain the rhythm.

"Mmm-mmm-mmm-mmm . . ." hummed Hawk.

He could tell Ms. Sasaki knew something was wrong. She watched him, wide-eyed. Did he sound terrible?

Get your focus back. He tried, but the beat slipped through his fingers like star glitter.

Suddenly the humming stopped with an abruptness that made Ben falter. Taking a quick breath, he listened. All he heard was dulcimer music. He kept going: "Fall on your knees. Oh, hear the angel voices."

He heard his voice grow strong again. He

smiled, winking at Ms. Sasaki. Relief colored her face like makeup.

Big finish, Garcia, he told himself. *Give it all you've got.*

"Oh-oh ni-ight. O night divi-i-i-i-i-i-i-ine!"

The auditorium exploded in applause. Applause that lasted a long, long time. Ben gave an embarrassed "pageant wave." Ms. Sasaki made him step off the risers and bow.

I did it!

When he climbed back to his place, he had a sudden urge to push a certain someone off the top step. But when he looked, Hawk was gone.

Uh-oh. Ben threw a glance backstage. The vampire was gone, too.

His heart began its kettledrum pound again. Only this time, for a different reason.

12.
Silent Night, Scary Night

We wish you a Merry Christmas, and a Happy New Year!"

Before applause for the last song died, Ben was off the back of the risers, heading for the stage door that led to the alley. Why did the disappearance of both Hawk and the vampire make him so nervous?

Had Zander cornered Hawk outside to tell him more bad jokes?

Right, Garcia.

Three steps from the door, Marly Thorn lunged in front of him. "Well? Aren't you going to thank me?"

"Thank you? For what?"

"Don't you know?" she huffed, looking insulted. "I saved your solo."

"What do you mean?"

"I'm the one who slipped off the risers and told your father what Hawk was doing to you. Then

your dad stepped in and — it was so cool, Ben,
you should have seen it. He lifted Hawk, like, with
one finger practically, and whisked him out the
door. I'll bet he's getting a real lecture right now."

So that's what happened. Thorn had saved him.

"Um, thanks, Thor — uh, Marly."

She tilted her head as if she didn't believe his
sincerity.

"No, I mean it. My solo was nose-diving because
of him. I . . . yeah, you helped me a lot. I really
mean it. Thank you."

Marly's friends were calling her. "Gotta go," she
said, backing away.

"Marly?" he called after her. "Merry Christmas."

Big smile. Jingle jingle. "Merry Christmas,
Ben."

Ben yanked off his robe, dumping it onto the
nearest chair. He rushed out the stage door —
smack into a pile of snow. Dashing outside without
his jacket was dumb, but he'd already wasted too
much time.

The moon was full; the air so cold, breathing
stung his nose.

He stepped across snowdrifts in the alley, heading into a field behind the school. Whimpering
sounds led him to a grove of blue spruce.

Hidden in the grove, Zander had Hawk backed

85

against the snowy boughs of a spruce.

Ben stopped to watch. What was Zander doing? He no longer wore Dad's clothes, but was back to full vampire attire. *How'd he do that?* Zander seemed able to do anything.

What he was doing to Hawk was terrorizing him. Ben circled the grove. Zander's fangs were down, shining white in the moonlight. He growled, more or less, at his pretend victim.

Hawk clawed at the branches, as if trying to make them surround and protect him. In his white choir robe, he looked like an angel in deep trouble.

The scene gave Ben a terrific idea.

He motioned to Zander to let him know he was there. Putting a finger to his lips, he mouthed, "Shhhhh."

Then Ben jumped between the vampire and Hawk. "Stop!" he shouted to Zander. "Don't hurt this boy."

"L-Look out!" Hawk tried to yell, but it came out a hoarse whisper. Shock whitened his face when he saw who'd come to save him.

Zander growled, swiping at Ben.

He twisted out of reach. "I know this boy deserves to be bitten," he shouted. "He's been cruel and mean to his fellow students."

"No," Hawk gasped. "Don't urge him on."

"He's nasty and he talks back to teachers."

"Please," Hawk whimpered. "Don't let him hurt me."

"He does things behind kids' backs, and *they* get blamed."

"I'm sorry, Garcia. Really, I am."

Zander attacked, grasping Hawk by the shoulders, with Ben caught in between. Hawk yowled like a three-year-old.

Ben twirled to clamp a hand over Hawk's mouth. The last thing he needed was someone hearing screams and dialing 911.

"I think," Ben snarled, pretending to shove Zander away with great effort. "I think the boy will mend his ways. Am I right?"

No answer. Unless you count whimpers as an answer.

"AM I RIGHT?" Ben yelled in Hawk's face.

"R-Right, man," Hawk said. "I'll never hassle you again. I promise."

Ben faced Zander, holding his arms like a school crossing guard. "I command you, in the name of all that is right and good, to leave us alone." He snapped his fingers. "Be gone!"

Fire crackled. Wind screamed. Somewhere a lone wolf howled.

Zander was gone.

Nice show, Zan. Ben could hardly keep from

laughing. What a great performance. For both of them.

He turned to Hawk. "Are you okay?"

Hawk was breathing as if he'd run twenty laps around the outfield. "I-I can't believe you did that."

"Well, I couldn't let him *get* you, could I? Not with it being Christmas and all."

"N-no, man, what you did was so great. I mean, you jumped between us and fought him off. I . . . hey, thanks, man. I owe you."

Ben shrugged. "Better get inside. You're getting your robe muddy. Ms. Sasaki won't like it."

Hawk looked down as if he'd just remembered what he was wearing. He attempted to brush off the muddy streaks, then gave up. "Hey, Garcia, I don't know how to tell you this, but I think that . . . that *thing* — whatever it was — got your dad. We came out here together, then . . . well, I don't know what happened to him. He sorta disappeared."

"Oh." Ben was relieved that Hawk hadn't connected his dad to the vampire. "Thanks, I'll scout around and see what I can find."

"You're crazy." Hawk squinted beyond the dark grove. "I'm gettin' outta here." He hustled away as if a phantom were chasing him.

Ben took a few steps. "Zan, are you here? He's gone."

"Behind you."

Ben jumped out of his skin and back in again. Zander leaned against a tree, not two feet away. "Don't scare me like that," Ben said.

Then he laughed, plowing through snow to shake the vampire's hand. "That was great, the way you cornered him and pretended to be a *real* vampire — I mean the *other* kind of vampire. You really scared him."

"I wasn't *trying* to scare the poor lad. I wanted to occupy him so he'd leave you be. Then I decided to — er — practice on him."

"Practice?"

Zander sighed, looking ashamed. "I was behaving the way I *used* to, in order to get ready for . . . well, it's been so long since I acted nasty and bloodthirsty. I was afraid The Big Guy might notice I'd gone soft if I didn't rehearse first."

Zander didn't move, didn't seem to be his old jovial self. The evil look on his face scared Ben. Literally. Ben felt as if he was in the presence of someone he didn't know. The uneasiness made him back away. "Hey, Zan, are you okay?"

"No." The vampire gazed toward the full moon. His eyes began to burn with a wicked, wicked light. The color of glowing coals. He turned his evil glare on Ben. "He has come," Zander whispered. "Tonight is the night."

Ben shivered, more from Zander's eerie words

than from the cold December night. "Oh, mith!" he cried. "Mith, mith, *mith!*"

Zander's eyes snapped back to normal. He sucked in a sharp breath, then stabbed a bony finger toward Ben. "Good Hades, young man, you'd better watch your tongue!"

13.
The Wrath of
The Big Guy

The ride home was quiet. Ben's mom seemed torn between wanting to yell at him for disappearing after the program, then showing up half-frozen without his jacket — or hugging him for making her proud.

Her words came to Ben through a fog. He was preoccupied, to say the least. He wished the night were normal. It *seemed* normal, creeping home in the truck on snow-packed roads, *oohing* and *aahing* at Christmas lights.

But his thoughts reminded him what lay ahead.

The scenario sounded like the blurb from a bad horror film: *He waits for you. A vampire. Not just any vampire, but one whose name is so powerful, all who say it are destroyed.*

Or melted, according to Zander.

Ben glanced at his mom. In her hooded, fuzzy coat, she looked like Mama Bear, heading home to her den to sleep away the rest of the winter.

He toyed with the idea of asking her if she believed in vampires. But he was afraid to say the word because, after tonight, he feared it might be screamed from the headlines of the *Woodrock News*.

If a real vampire arrived in Woodrock, wasn't it logical that he would have to feed? Ben doubted the vampire's mother packed him a lunch for the trip. He'd have to feed *here*. On humans.

If Zander and I face this guy, only one of us qualifies as a real, live human — Me! I'M THE ONE THE KING OF THE UNDEAD WILL WANT!

"Dear? Are you listening?"

"Huh?"

"I said, let's go on to the airport instead of going home. Your dad's plane isn't due for another hour, but the airport's a long way, and the roads are bad. We need to head on out there right now."

And be gone the rest of the evening? Zander would never forgive him. Didn't seem like a good idea to anger someone immortal.

"Gee, Mom, do you mind dropping me off at home? I'm, uh, kind of tired after the program and all."

"You're tired?" she repeated. "It's Friday night. You're on vacation for two weeks. And your dad's coming home." She reached to muss his hair. "Good grief, Ben, get a life."

Panic trickled down his spine. "Seriously, Mom, I need to go home."

"Why?"

"Well, I'm, uh, reading this really good book, and I'm almost to the end." He *was* reading a good book, so his words were true. He just hadn't had much time to read in the past few days.

"Okay, you win." She turned off the main highway, and backtracked toward home. "Must be a great book. What's it about?"

"Vampires." The word leaped from his lips before he could stop it. He waited for her reaction.

"Oh," was all she said.

Heck, he didn't need to *read* a book about vampires. At this point, he could *write* one.

At home, Ben jumped from the truck. His mother's instructions followed him up the porch steps: "Keep the doors locked. Don't wait up for us. And, look — someone left the light on in the attic; please turn it off."

Ben stopped by his room to get his bookbag full of Christmas gifts from the Elf Bazaar. Licorice was curled in a ball on his bed. He picked her up and hugged her. "Good-bye, Lic," he whispered into her fur. "I'll be back soon. I *promise* I'll come back." He refused to let his mind dwell on any deeper meaning his good-bye signified.

At the top of the attic stairs, Ben hesitated. Was it safe to enter? Was The Big Guy waiting to grab him? Wrestle him to the ground? Sink his fangs into Ben's neck?

"The light's on," he whispered to the door. "How can he be here if the light's on?" Ben pushed the door open. "Zan?"

"Enter," came Zander's voice.

Ben entered. The vampire, wearing dark glasses, stood with his traveling bag slung over one shoulder. His corner had been emptied of personal belongings — and tidied up.

"Are you leaving? Where are you going? Why is the light on?" The questions tumbled over each other as Ben tried to get them all out. Suddenly the idea of the vampire going away left him with a twinge of sadness. His dad left all the time, and now Zander was leaving.

The vampire motioned for Ben to come closer and sit. He slumped his traveling bag to the floor, then perched on it.

"I'm befuddled, Benjamin. I know The Big Guy's *here*, but I don't know *where*. I turned on the light to prevent him from making an appearance in the attic. But it's too bright for my comfort. I found these dark glasses on your father's dresser, so I borrowed them."

"They make you look cool," Ben joked. But the joke fell flat.

"I've never left an assignment without the Boss giving me permission and telling me where to go next. Now my plan is simply to flee. He will follow, of course, or send his evil servants after me. But if I keep moving, never staying in one place, maybe I can evade them — for a while."

Zander sighed. "The *problem* is that I cannot leave until my family arrives. The message I sent will guide them *here*. I must wait for them, even if it means The Big Guy finds me first."

He wrung his gloved hands. "I did so want to show Layla that spot in the forest. The spot where, I thought, we might build a cottage and put down roots. I do so want roots. I'm not the type to flee around the world. I like to stay in one place. That's why I dearly miss my home in Multiveinia."

What can I say to make him feel better? "Would it help if you showed *me* your spot in the forest?" Ben asked. The idea of having the entire vampire family settle nearby intrigued him. He could visit Zander Junior and Zandra. Maybe they could teach him how to zip from place to place in seconds.

Zander put a hand to his cheek, touched. "You want to see my special place?"

Ben nodded. "Is it safe to go outside? We could take the flashlight."

"We could," Zander agreed. "And this." He stepped back to his corner to retrieve the one thing he'd left behind. The jar of garlic cloves. He tossed it to Ben as if it was burning his hand.

"*I* know." Ben turned the lid. "We can string some around our necks — "

"DON'T OPEN THE JAR!" The only part of Zander's face that had color — his lips — lost it.

Ben tightened the lid. "You told me garlic didn't bother you anymore."

"Well, I can hold the bottle for short periods of time, but I cannot uncap it. Reversing a centuries-old curse takes time, dear boy."

Ben shoved the garlic into his backpack, on top of the gifts so it'd be easy to reach.

The color returned to Zander's lips. "I suppose I should try all the — uh — *remedies* for vampires to see if I'm desensitized to others. You don't have any s-s-s . . ." He paused, as if getting up nerve to say the word. "Any s-s-*stakes* in the house, do you?" He crinkled his brow, waiting for the reply.

"We don't eat meat," Ben said.

"The *pointed* kind of stakes, dear boy."

"Oh." Ben shook his head.

Zander picked up his traveling bag, glancing sorrowfully about the attic, as if saying good-bye to his home. Taking off the dark glasses, he set them down, then grasped Ben's arm. When he let go, cold air slapped Ben's face. They were in the middle of the forest.

Ben was prepared this time, with jacket and

gloves. He took the garlic from his backpack and held it in one hand, just in case. Zander turned on the flashlight, holding a glove over it to keep it from shining too brightly.

"Here is where I'd build," Zander said, twirling in the clearing. "My V.A.M.P. colleagues would form a bat cloud and come together to help me finish the cottage in one night."

"It's nice here," Ben told him. Moonlight filtered through tall pines, circling the area like castle guards.

Ben brushed snow off a rock and sat. "You never told me what The Big Guy might do when he catches up to you," he said. "I mean, he can't exactly murder you, right?"

"There are worse things than murder." Zander glanced about the clearing with great sadness. "I've spent centuries earning seniority at Ghastly Castle. There are many ranks of vampires. Seniority allows more freedom, like the freedom to go off on assignments around the world. The Big Guy knows where we are, and *assumes* we're following orders, but he has no way of knowing if we don't.

"So we, the VAMPs, take assignments to spread goodwill instead of pain and suffering. If The Big Guy strips my seniority, I'll have to return to the castle, and remain there doing his dirty work."

"Dirty work?"

"Well, I might be assigned to the crew who finds victims for The Big Guy. Or I might be relegated to the ranks of those who make sure the castle is kept dirty, disheveled, and full of spiders and cobwebs. Make sure the floorboards remain creaky, the railings loose, and the stairways missing steps here and there. And keep the lightning flashing, thunder crashing, and rain coming in torrents."

"Wow." Ben was astounded.

"Well, *somebody* has to do it. That was my job back in the 1600s when I first arrived there. But I flew through the ranks with 'great promise,' according to Uncle Okvaldo. He, too, was a seventh son, and took me under his wing — if you'll pardon the pun. He was one of the founders of V.A.M.P., and was responsible for my conversion."

"Where is he now?"

"Still at Ghastly Castle. He's our contact there. It's a well-kept secret, of course. If The Big Guy ever found out, Uncle Okvaldo might receive the worst punishment of all."

"Which is?"

"Which is — losing one's head and being cursed to walk the earth for eternity as a hideous, headless monster, constantly craving nourishment, but unable to get it. So you see why it's terribly important that The Big Guy never finds out."

In a heartbeat, the moon blinked out, spreading blackness across the earth.

Then a deafening rumble that sounded like an earthquake, but was really a heavily accented voice, thundered, "Well, thank you so much for telling me."

14.
Silver Fangs, Silver Fangs, Soon It Will Be Christmas Day

A cyclone was born with Ben in its eye.

Hugging his backpack, he squeezed his eyes shut as the funnel whirled madly around him. Blackness from the other side of the stars was sucked down the funnel, wrapping him in a darkness deeper than night.

The word *frightened* seemed far too mild for the terror streaking through his blood. "Zander!" he screamed. "What's happening?"

The cyclone rose, swallowing snow from the surrounding ground, turning the dark into a whiteness that stung his eyes.

Then it was gone.

Ben blinked, jumping to look in every direction, tensed to fight or run. But running seemed pointless. How far would he get? Besides, he couldn't leave Zander.

The ground and trees around him were now devoid of snow. Moonlight trickled back to earth, toned down from its original brightness. Ben found Zander. He was sealed in a glass box, seven feet high.

Ben circled the box, searching for a way to free his friend. Zander's face was beyond sad. He made no attempt to escape.

"You've got to try!" Ben shouted, wondering if his voice carried through the glass.

"It's no use," came a voice from behind.

Ben whirled. Before him stood another vampire. If Zander was seven feet tall, this guy was eight. His hair was long, slicked back in a ponytail, with sideburns that grew across his pale face, meeting under his nose in a mustache.

His ears were more pointed than bat ears, his fingernails long, each filed to a point. One ear sported an earring shaped like a dagger dripping blood. And, even though the moonlight painted shadows across the clearing, no shadow sprang from the vampire's form.

"Why did you do this to him?" Ben yelled, then wished he hadn't. After all, if the vampire standing before him was The Big Guy, so powerful he could remove snow from the area simply to make it darker, why anger him?

"Your friend, Alexander Carpathian, is packaged, ready for shipment back to the old country." He didn't appear offended by Ben's yelling.

"But he can't breathe in there."

The vampire's laughter colored the wind with evil. Ben preferred Zander's laugh, as odd as it was. "What makes you think he depends on *air* for life?"

Ben shivered. *Think, Garcia. This guy could do away with you in an instant, then snap his fingers and send Zander hurtling back to Multiveinia.*

The great idea he'd had in English class this morning suddenly seemed lame out here, facing the Emperor of Doom.

Ben glanced at Zander, who seemed comatose. He offered no help at all. It was up to Ben.

The vampire circled the clearing, like a panther studying his prey. "You realize what's going to happen now, don't you?"

"No." Ben's mind refused to imagine the immediate future.

"Well then, let me tell you." The vampire's circle grew smaller, tightening around Ben like the cyclone. "First, I will have a light snack. You're so puny, I can't consider you a feast. But I *will* feast tonight."

He planted himself firmly in front of Ben. "I didn't catch your name, lad. May I call you *appetizer?*"

Ben thought it best not to answer. Besides, his tongue was stuck between his teeth, clenched to keep from chattering.

"I will find my feast nearby. And, I think a certain black cat will make a tasty after-dinner snack."

He knows where I live! Ben thought about his parents. He knew *his* life was in jeopardy, but he never considered the possibility that his *parents'* lives might be in danger, too. He could *not* let this happen.

The vampire grinned. Fangs slid into place. Silver fangs, instead of white ones like Zander's. They seemed as long as walrus tusks.

Ben cleared his throat. "I brought you something," he said, trying hard to quench the wiggle in his voice.

"You brought me something?" The Big Guy cocked his head to one side, stepping back in caution. "Ah, you've done your homework."

"My homework?"

"So, what is it? Are you going to flash a mirror and drive me away? Do you have a sharp stake hidden in your pocket? A handful of garlic to toss in my face?"

The vampire threw back his head and roared. Literally. The force threw Ben against a tree trunk. The tree vibrated. He hung on. The whole effect sounded like thunder, which seemed out of place in December.

The Big Guy folded his body in half and put his ghost-white face close to Ben's. "Don't you think

I've had a lion's share of mirrors thrust in my face over the years? Listen." Leaning closer, he whispered, "I can shatter the glass with nothing more than a wink."

Ben shuddered. The vampire smelled like old clothes packed in a trunk for a few hundred years.

"Don't you think anyone has tried to drive a stake through my heart? *Thousands* have, lad. And — here *I* am. Where do you suppose *they* are?"

His leering grin was answer enough.

"And garlic? It would take a *field* of garlic to affect me. I've lived for centuries. *You*, lad, are no more than a leaf. Full of young life, yet gone by the end of the season. And . . ." He paused to uncurl five knife-blade fingernails in Ben's face. "This is the end of your season."

"B-But, sir," Ben said, gulping. "I didn't bring you any of those things."

"Oh, no?" He feigned surprise. "Then what are you hiding in your hand? Could it be . . . garlic?"

Whoops. Ben had forgotten about the garlic. During the terror of the last fifteen minutes, the jar had practically seared itself into his hand.

"Don't you think I know what great plans you have?"

"You've got to believe me," Ben pleaded. "I brought you something *nice*. Something you will like. *This* is not it." Stepping back, he flung the jar of garlic in the opposite direction. As it disappeared over a rocky mound, he remembered, with a pang of regret, that it was one of a matching set of spice jars he'd given to Mom last Christmas.

The vampire's expression changed — first to disbelief at Ben's action, then to curiosity and mistrust. "You brought me something *nice?*"

Ben nodded.

"You mean, you knew we'd be having this — er — *tête-à-tête?*"

"Oh, yes," Ben answered, although he wasn't quite sure what *tête-à-tête* meant. "I knew you were coming." He glanced at the glass cage. A mortified Zander stared toward the rocky mound, as if he couldn't believe Ben had thrown away his only weapon against certain death.

Ben sighed. *Okay, Garcia, you got yourself into this. Stick to the plan. It's your only hope.* Imitating Zander's bow, he extended a hand. "I'm very pleased to meet you, Mr., uh, sir."

The vampire raised his bushy eyebrows. "You're pleased to meet *me? Nobody* is pleased to meet me. Ever." He walked away, as if trying to remember if he'd encountered this sort of thing in the past. "What did you bring me?" he asked from a distance.

"Christmas presents."

"You're teasing."

"No." Ben retrieved his backpack, then scouted

the area until he found a small evergreen sapling. One by one, he pulled out the gaily wrapped presents and arranged them under the tree.

Feeling the vampire's eyes on him, Ben took his time. The pile of gifts looked bright and inviting, but the bare tree was depressing. Christmas decorations were badly needed.

A few pine cones lay scattered on the ground. Ben collected them, placing the cones gently in the branches.

He sorted through his jacket pockets and found: two red movie ticket stubs, the last four shopping lists Mom had given him, and a glittery yellow star she'd saved from the Christmas program.

Ben smoothed the star and placed it on top of the tree, wrapping the string around the branches to secure it. He set the red ticket stubs on branches, then wadded Mom's shopping lists into balls and added them.

In his jeans pocket, he found a comb, his last dollar, and six baseball cards. He arranged them neatly on the branches. Stepping back, he admired his impromptu task. *Not bad, Garcia.*

Ben was so caught up in what he was doing, he almost forgot the King of the Undead was breathing down his neck.

The vampire sat on the ground, a thoughtful look on his face as he studied the "decorated" tree. "You did this for me?"

"Yes, sir. Part of Christmas is sharing gifts with people you like, and — "

The Big Guy snorted. "Now, you're telling me you *like* me?"

Ben hated to lie. "You've been very, um, honest, sir." It was the only truth he could come up with. "You see, Christmas is — "

"I know what Christmas is, lad. I've been around long enough to figure it out. I usually take the week off because there's entirely too much goodwill in the world. Gives me the creeps."

He stood, straightening his cape. "If you've finished your little show, I will feed and be on my way."

Ben's knees knocked. It wasn't working. "But, sir, you haven't opened your presents yet."

"Well, all right. Which one is mine?"

"All of them."

"All of them? All those gifts are *mine?*" He clasped his hands together as though Ben had promised him daylight would never come again.

Ben picked up a medium-sized box wrapped in shiny green paper sprinkled with red-and-white candy canes. "Here."

The vampire plopped to the ground again, settling his cape around his spider legs. He ripped off the wrapping paper, holding up a set of four toy cars, each a different color, with racing stripes and numbers on the sides.

"Oh!" he exclaimed, acting truly delighted. "Toys! I never had toys growing up. My family was poor, you know. Papa died when I was three, and Mum worked making hats for noble ladies, so there was never any — "

He stopped, glancing at Ben in embarrassment. "Never any toys — or presents — for that matter."

"You had Christmas?" Ben blurted. "I mean, I didn't think vampires — "

"I haven't always been a vampire, lad. Not all of us are seventh sons, like Alexander."

Zander was watching the scene with wide-eyed fascination.

"Give me more presents," The Big Guy demanded.

Ben played Santa while the vampire opened one gift after another, acting thrilled over each one:

"A book about planets! I've always wanted to learn about the sky.

"Wool socks! My feet are always cold in that drafty castle.

"A box of pencils! Perfect for recording my thoughts.

"A manicure set. Splendid! I never have enough nail files.

"A set of baseball cards!" He studied them with a curious look on his face. "What are *these* for?"

By the time the last gift was opened, Ben had

heard The Big Guy's life story: How he'd fallen victim to a she-vampire when he stayed out too late against his mum's wishes.

How he'd run away from Ghastly Castle so many times, Count Nikovich had him thrown into the dungeon.

How, in the dungeon, a dying seer had told him three secret truths the next Count of Ghastly Castle must know to become Czar of all Vampires.

And how, when the search began for a new count, *he* was the only one who knew the three secret truths.

Ben was fascinated by the vampire's stories, but his mind warned him not to become complacent. The battle wasn't won yet.

"No more?" The vampire pouted in disappointment.

Ben wished he'd had more money for gifts. "No sir," he apologized. "I'm sorry."

The vampire stood. All the Christmas presents and colored ribbons disappeared into hidden pockets inside his cape. He folded the wrapping paper into neat squares and saved it, too. Then he began to cry.

Ben was shocked. Tears? From the Emperor of Doom?

"No one has shown me this much kindness since Mum, lad. I'll truly never forget you."

"Does this mean . . . ?" Ben was afraid to ask

for his and Zander's freedom.

"It means I will feel absolutely terrible after biting your neck because you are the first person who ever gave me Christmas. My first tree, my first toys." Sniffle sniffle.

Ben's blood ran hot and cold. "So, why do you have to go through with the rest of it? I mean, I was nice to you, but in return . . ." He couldn't get the words out.

"I don't know what *else* to do." The Big Guy paced. His cape, heavy with gifts, tangled about his legs. "I've never let a victim get away. Not in four hundred years. I mean, I can't. I could *tell* you to run for your life — even give you a head start, but I would fly right after you. It's instinct. Run from a bear and he will chase and devour you. Nature is as nature does."

"You mean, after showing you the true meaning of Christmas," Ben said in a fuzzy whisper, "I'm still doomed?"

The King of the Undead grinned. Silver fangs, cold and sharp, slid into place, ready for the attack. "Doomed?" he repeated. "Doomed is a good way of putting it. . . ."

15.
It's Beginning to Look a Lot Like Curtains

Ben hung his head. He'd failed.

The pride and success that had swelled his heart after he sang his solo took a bungee jump all the way down to hopelessness and despair.

His life, his good intentions, meant nothing now. He'd failed Zander. His parents, too. They were in mortal danger and didn't even know it.

And poor Licorice.

A whimper escaped from Ben's throat. He pulled himself tall. He would *not* stand here and whimper like Hawk. Hadn't he put up a good fight? Why did he ever think he could outwit the Czar, the Emperor, the King? A supernatural creature with a few hundred years' experience?

Ben stepped closer to Zander's prison, placing his palm against the cold glass.

Zander did the same. "Good-bye, my son," he said, wiping a tear.

"Good-bye, my friend," Ben answered.

Suddenly Zander's gaze was drawn over Ben's head. His eyes grew as large and oval as Christmas ornaments.

The Big Guy is preparing to attack.

For a moment, Ben couldn't move. But his mind told him to turn around. Why make it easy on the vampire? Why let him attack from the back without seeing his victim's eyes? A victim who'd just given him Christmas.

Ben took two steps to the side, hopping on top of an outcropping of rock. The vampire whooshed past, missing him, smashing into the glass.

Ben faced his attacker. Only one thing would make him feel strong again. He began to sing. "O holy night . . ."

The vampire froze, arms out, mouth open, fangs in position.

"The stars are brightly shining . . ."

"No!" The Big Guy shouted. "Stop!"

Ben did not obey. He kept singing.

"Not Christmas carols! Please!" The vampire waved his hands, jumping from one side of Ben's rock to the other, as if the song had placed Ben in a glass box, too, and the vampire couldn't penetrate it.

As long as Ben kept singing.

"A thrill of hope, the weary world rejoices."

"Mum sang to me — in the cradle, on her lap —

on the night, oh, that fateful night, I disobeyed was Christmas Eve. The last time I saw Mum, she was standing by the hearth, singing, singing a Christmas carol."

The Big Guy dropped to one knee. "Please, lad," he begged. "I beseech you to desist."

Ben paused. "I'll stop singing if you'll let Zander and me go — peacefully."

The vampire scowled. His eyes shot fiery sparks.

"And if you free Zander from his assignments, and let him live where he wants to."

"Well, I — "

"And if you do nothing to harm Uncle Okvaldo."

The vampire rose, until all eight feet of him met Ben eye to eye on his rock. "This is highly irregular."

"For yonder breaks a new and glorious morn!"

"I cannot grant your request!"

"Fall on your knees . . ."

The vampire fell on his knees, covering his pointed ears with both hands. "Yes, yes, *yes!* I'll do what you ask. Now *STOP!*" The word thundered past Ben, ripping bare branches off trees.

Ben obeyed.

A wind kicked up and the moon brightened. The glass prison melted with a tinkling of chimes.

Zander flew to Ben's side, pointing a finger at The Big Guy. "In the name of all that is horrible

113

and despicable, I bind you to your word."

"Yeah, yeah, yeah." The Big Guy stalked off, disgusted. At the edge of the clearing, he stopped. "Alexander," he snapped in a voice that didn't seem as threatening as before. "I release you from my service. I will not bother you for seven generations."

"But —"

Zander jabbed Ben in the ribs to shut him up.

"Do not breathe a word of this to anyone," he commanded.

"Who would I tell?" Ben said.

Zander poked him in the ribs again. "Hush!"

The Big Guy sneered at Ben in disgust. "Twentieth-century kids," he muttered. "Blah."

He pointed at Zander. "One more thing. Send word to Okvaldo to be gone before I return to Ghastly Castle. If he's there when I arrive, he'll receive the full extent of my wrath. If he's gone, I'll release him, too, from my service."

Zander bowed in acknowledgment.

A cyclone sprang from the ground. Ben grabbed Zander and held on. Lightning crackled. Thunder rattled the earth. The Big Guy was gone.

"Whew," they both said at the same time.

"You're free!" Ben cried. "What will you do now? Where will you go?"

Zander smiled a no-fang smile. "I'm not leaving.

This is where I'll build my cottage. This is where my roots will grow deep."

"But what if someone happens by?"

"They'll see trees and rocks, flowers in the springtime, snow in winter. But no one will see the cottage. Unless I want them to."

"What about your family? When will they arrive?"

Zander lifted his head and listened to the wind, the way Licorice did when Ben let her outside. "Soon. They will be here soon."

His melancholy smile told Ben how much the vampire missed his family.

"In a few nights," Zander continued, "you will have a dream. In it you will come for a visit at a cottage in the forest, and I will welcome you, along with Layla and the twins and Uncle Okvaldo. The dream will be my invitation to you, so please come."

"I will," Ben said. "As long as you don't call me *appetizer*."

Zander sucked in his breath, appalled. "Really, Benjamin, that's *not* funny." He gave his elegant bow. "How can I ever, ever thank you?"

"Don't tell any more jokes to my friends."

Zander didn't seem to understand. He lifted his head again, listening. "Your parents are nearing Meadow Lane. Let's get you home to bed."

He reached for Ben's arm.

"Wait." Ben had one more thing to say. "Welcome to Woodrock, Zan. May I be the first to wish you a Merry Christmas?"

"Thank you," the vampire returned. "And a Joyous Noel to you and your family." Then he pinched Ben's arm.

Ben fluffed his pillow, listening to the truck tires crunching snow below his bedroom window. Licorice hopped onto his bed.

Humming, "Jingle bats, jingle bats, Zander's going to stay," Ben planned what he'd buy the twins for Christmas — if Dad would take him shopping and give him an advance on his allowance.

Sure he will; it's Christmas.

Hugging his cat, Ben snuggled under the covers. And then he settled down for a long winter's nap.

About the Author

Dian Curtis Regan is the author of many books for young readers, including *My Zombie Valentine*, *Liver Cookies*, and *The Kissing Contest*. Ms. Regan enjoyed researching vampires for this book until she learned that those born with red hair were once thought to be vampires. Being born with red hair herself, she is relieved this belief no longer exists — yet it *does* explain the extensive dental work her parents put her through.

A native of Colorado Springs, Ms. Regan lives and writes (mostly at night) in Edmond, Oklahoma.